Trapped!

They had taken less than a dozen steps into the cave when Nog's foot crunched on something. He stopped to pick it up.

"What is it?" Jake asked.

"I don't think you want to know," Nog replied as he held the object up so that it caught the wan light streaming through the cave entrance.

Jake took it from Nog's hand. The Ferengi was right. He *didn't* want to know what it was.

What Jake held in his hand was a piece of bone that something had obviously feasted upon. And the moistness told Jake that it had not been very long ago. . . .

He heard it again. The sound that had awoken him.

It was coming from deeper in the cave. A kind of soft padding. Something was in the cave with them—and it was coming in their direction!

Star Trek: The Next Generation
STARFLEET ACADEMY

Star Trek: Deep Space Nine

Star Trek movie tie-in

Star Trek Generations

Available from MINSTREL Books

STAR TREK
DEEP SPACE NINE®

GYPSY WORLD

TED PEDERSEN

Interior illustrations by
Todd Cameron Hamilton

A MINSTREL® BOOK

PUBLISHED BY POCKET BOOKS

New York   London   Toronto   Sydney   Tokyo   Singapore

A MINSTREL PAPERBACK *Original*

A Minstrel Book published by
POCKET BOOKS, a division of Simon & Schuster Inc.
1230 Avenue of the Americas, New York, NY 10020

A VIACOM COMPANY

STAR TREK is a Registered Trademark of Paramount Pictures.

This book is published by Pocket Books, a division of Simon & Schuster Inc., under exclusive license from Paramount Pictures.

ISBN: 0-671-51115-7

First Minstrel Books printing February 1996

10 9 8 7 6 5 4 3 2 1

A MINSTREL BOOK and colophon are registered trademarks of Simon & Schuster Inc.

Cover art by Alan Gutierrez

Printed in the U.S.A.

*For David Alexander, good friend
and fellow Trekker*

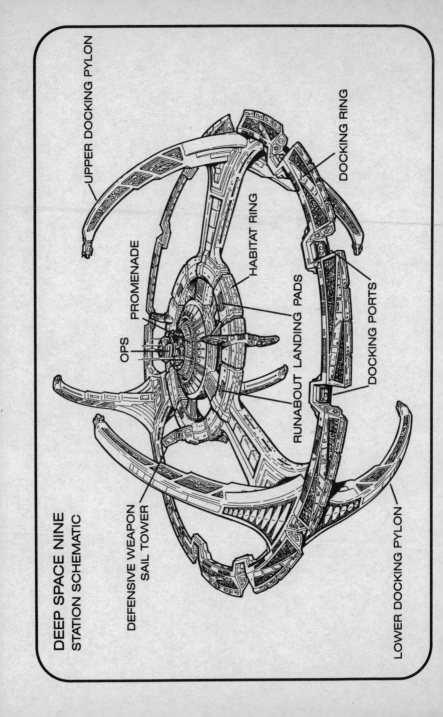

DEEP SPACE NINE
STATION SCHEMATIC

UPPER DOCKING PYLON

DOCKING RING

HABITAT RING

PROMENADE

OPS

RUNABOUT LANDING PADS

DOCKING PORTS

DEFENSIVE WEAPON
SAIL TOWER

LOWER DOCKING PYLON

STAR TREK®: DEEP SPACE NINE™

Cast of Characters

JAKE SISKO—Jake is a young teenager and the only human boy permanently on board Deep Space Nine. Jake's mother died when he was very young. He came to the space station with his father but found very few kids his own age. He doesn't remember life on Earth, but he loves baseball and candy bars, and he hates homework. His father doesn't approve of his friendship with Nog.

NOG—He is a Ferengi boy whose primary goal in life—like all Ferengi—is to make money. His father, Rom, is frequently away on business, which is fine with Nog. His uncle, Quark, keeps an eye on him. Nog thinks humans are odd with their notions of trust and favors and friendship. He doesn't always understand Jake, but since his father forbids him to hang out with the human boy, Nog and Jake are best friends. Nog loves to play tricks on people, but he tries to avoid Odo whenever possible.

COMMANDER BENJAMIN SISKO—Jake's father has been appointed by Starfleet Command to oversee the operations of the space station and act as a liaison between the Federation and Bajor. His wife was killed in a Borg attack, and he is raising Jake by himself. He is a very busy man who always tries to make time for his son.

ODO—The security officer was found by Bajoran scientists years ago, but Odo has no idea where he originally came from. He is a shape-shifter, and thus can assume any shape for a period of time. He normally maintains a vaguely human appearance but every sixteen hours he must revert to his natural liquid state. He has no patience for lawbreakers and less for Ferengi.

MAJOR KIRA NERYS—Kira was a freedom fighter in the Bajoran underground during the Cardassian occupation of Bajor. She now represents Bajoran interests aboard the station and is Sisko's first officer. Her temper is legendary.

LIEUTENANT JADZIA DAX—An old friend of Commander Sisko's, the science officer Dax is actually two joined entities known as the Trill. There is a separate consciousness—a symbiont—in the young female host's body. Sisko knew the symbiont Dax in a previous host, which was a "he."

DR. JULIAN BASHIR—Eager for adventure, Doctor Bashir graduated at the top of his class and requested a deep-space posting. His enthusiasm sometimes gets him into trouble.

MILES O'BRIEN—Formerly the Transporter Chief aboard the *U.S.S. Enterprise,* O'Brien is now Chief of Operations on Deep Space Nine.

KEIKO O'BRIEN—Keiko was a botanist on the *Enterprise,* but she moved to the station with her husband and her young daughter, Molly. Since there is little use for her botany skills on the station, she is the teacher for all of the permanent and traveling students.

QUARK—Nog's uncle and a Ferengi businessman by trade, Quark runs his own combination restaurant/casino/holosuite venue on the Promenade, the central meeting place for much of the activity on the station. Quark has his hand in every deal on board and usually manages to stay just one step ahead of the law—usually in the shape of Odo.

Historian's note: The events of this series take place during the first and second seasons of the *Deep Space Nine* television show.

GYPSY WORLD

CHAPTER 1

Jake stared at the man. He knew that it was rude, but he couldn't help it. He had never seen a Fjori before. The Fjori was big and possessed a heavy beard. His face was tanned and scarred from the burning rays of a hundred suns and the winds of a thousand worlds. His clothes were loose-fitting, yet he wore them with the same pride that Jake's father wore his Starfleet dress uniform.

Commander Benjamin Sisko nudged his son, and Jake quickly averted his eyes as the man approached. Sisko offered his hand in a greeting. "Welcome to Deep Space Nine, Captain Vardk. I'm Commander Sisko. This is my son, Jake."

Captain Jrl Vardk of the star trader *Orak* accepted Sisko's handshake with a firm grip. He nodded at Jake. "I appreciate your allowing us the use of your repair facilities, Commander."

"Deep Space Nine is here to accommodate any ship traveling through the Bajoran Wormhole."

"Even a *Fjori* ship?"

Sisko smiled. "My own ancestors suffered centuries of prejudice on Old Earth. We have that in common."

Vardk nodded, then added, "But you, at least, no longer have to endure the wrath of your fellows."

"As long as the Fjori choose to remain outside the system, there will be those who distrust you."

"You are right, of course, but the people of the *Orak,* like the Gypsies of your own planet, are destined to be nomads. To forever wander the starways."

"If that is your choice."

"That is how it has been since the beginning of our history. It cannot be otherwise." Vardk spoke as though it were an undisputed truth.

With that, the captain of the *Orak* turned and walked away. He was almost to the airlock when he stopped, turned and looked back at Sisko. "I suggest that for your peace of mind as well as my own, you put this docking bay off limits while we are here."

"I've already ordered that," Sisko replied. "You have my word that you will not be disturbed while you and your family are guests on Deep Space Nine."

Jake watched Captain Vardk disappear around a corner, then he turned to his father. "Does that mean we can't visit the Fjori ship?"

"I'm afraid it does, Jake. The Fjori are a very private people, and I want to honor their wishes. Docking bay seven is off limits to everyone while they are here." He gave Jake a sharp look. "That applies to you and your friend Nog."

* * *

Even though it was the weekend, as soon as Jake left his father, he headed for the space station's school.

Actually, to call it a "school" was charitable. Keiko O'Brien had converted an empty shop into a classroom, complete with personal computers for the half-dozen station children who were her students.

Jake had initially complained to his father that putting the "little kids" in the same class as the teenagers like Nog and himself was not really proper. But Benjamin Sisko had explained that "one-room schoolhouses" had been the norm in the frontier days on Earth. And Deep Space Nine was definitely the frontier in the 24th century.

Like most things his father told him, Jake accepted it—then went on to research the subject on his own. Usually he found that his father was right.

At the moment what Jake was interested in researching was the Fjori. He set his computer to the task and waited for the results.

He did not have to wait long.

"Search complete," the feminine voice of the computer proclaimed. Jake had once asked his father why most computer voices were female. His father thought about it a moment, then replied that it might be because the voice of a woman seemed less threatening than that of a man. Since computers, in their early years, were strange and even frightening to many people, perhaps they were given the more comforting voice of a woman.

4

It made sense to Jake. Even now when he remembered the soft voice of his mother, bad times were easier to endure.

"Display results," Jake commanded the computer.

A holographic starmap materialized in the front of the room. Jake recognized it as Gamma Quadrant. He expected to see colored dots of light superimposed over the map to represent the Fjori starships in the quadrant. But there were no dots. "Where are the Fjori ships?" he asked.

"The number of Fjori in the charted universe is not known, since only a few have passed through the wormhole in the two years of its operation," the computer reported. "There is insufficient statistical records in the data files upon which to make a reliable estimate."

"Why is that?" Jake asked.

"Fjori are nomadic. No record exists of their colonizing a planet, owning a territory, forming a government, or fighting a war. No official records exist because the Fjori themselves have never submitted to a census."

"In other words," Jake summed up, "they don't talk about themselves."

"Correct," the computer confirmed. "There is no reliable data on the Fjori in the files."

"There must be something."

The starmap changed to focus on a cluster of stars, and on a particular star near the outer edge of the galactic cluster.

"Is that the Fjori home world?" he asked.

"It is a simulation based on legends and folk tales," replied the computer. "There is no verified record of the location of their home planet. It is not certain that it still exists.

"It is believed that after centuries of wandering across their planet, with the advent of the starship they migrated to the remote regions of space. Here they continued their nomadic ways. They became traders, traveling from world to world—venturing out to the farthest regions of the universe. Their starships —like their wagons of previous centuries—are their only real homes."

"Computer. Shut up."

The computer obeyed and the starmap vanished. Jake turned to face the interruption—his Ferengi friend, Nog.

"Why'd you do that?" Jake wanted to know.

"'Cause if you want to know all about Fjori, you're not going to find it in some musty database."

"Oh. So you're an expert on the subject?"

"I am." Nog flashed a broad smile, the way he did when he was particularly pleased with himself. "In fact, I know quite a bit about the Fjori that isn't even in the computer."

Jake had learned to take Nog's boasts with more than a grain of salt. "Such as?" he challenged.

Nog stepped close and put his arm around Jake's shoulder, the way he had seen his uncle Quark do when he was about to sell some unsuspecting spacer a share in a Durellian mine in the Lost Quadrant. "I know the way to the secret Fjori home world."

There was a long pause. Jake broke the silence. "Well. Are you going to tell me?"

There was another pause before Nog smiled. "For a price."

CHAPTER 2

It was crowded on the Promenade. Seven ships were in port besides the *Orak,* and the shops were busy. And no place was busier than Quark's.

Jake and Nog weren't allowed inside, of course, but they could observe most of the action from one of the kiosks, the small open booths that overlooked the main concourse.

"I've never heard of the Fjori world," Jake said as he munched on his jumja—otherwise referred to by the locals as "glop on a stick."

"Are you naive or are you naive," Nog commented. He had already finished his own snack, the "price" he had demanded for his information. For a moment he contemplated trying for a second "glop," but thought better of it. Jake was an easy mark, but he was also just about the only real friend that Nog had. "The Fjori world is the secret planet where Fjori go once every five years for their Gathering."

"If it's a secret," Jake wondered, "how do you know where it is?"

Nog leaned over and whispered. "I don't actually know exactly where it is—but I know how to find out."

"How?"

"The Fjori starmaps."

"Oh. You're just going to walk up to Captain Vardk and ask him to show you their maps?"

"Well . . . not exactly. There is another way."

Jake knew what that was. "You're not going to try and steal them?"

Nog feigned shock at such a notion. "Steal? No. Just sneak a quick look."

"Don't even think about it," Jake cautioned. "My dad's put the Fjori docking bay off limits."

Nog leaned back in his chair and said nothing.

Jake knew perfectly well that his Ferengi friend was plotting to get into Docking Bay seven. And he was determined not to get involved in another of Nog's schemes.

Nog saw the situation somewhat differently. As a people, Ferengi were not normally bound by rules. In fact, they generally considered the only reason to have a rule was so that a Ferengi could break it. On the other hand, even his uncle Quark found it unwise to go against Benjamin Sisko.

The station commander was a fair man—unless his rules were violated. Then his wrath was terrible enough to intimidate even a Klingon. On the other hand, Nog knew that his status in the eyes of his uncle and the other Ferengis would soar if he acquired those Fjori starmaps. And he knew there would be an opportunity. Nog only hoped he had the brains to see it and the courage to grasp it.

For the moment, Nog turned his attention to the evening's activity on the Promenade . . . where the opportunity the young Ferengi wanted was about to happen.

That opportunity wore the olive-skinned looks and the colorful tunic of a Fjori trader. His name, as they would learn, was Kala, and he was only a few years older than Jake or Nog. He was trying to grow a beard, as did most male Fjori, but so far the attempt had not been particularly successful.

It was doubtful that he was old enough to be in Quark's, but the enterprising Ferengi barkeeper was never one to ask questions when it might cost him a paying customer.

Kala took a stool at the end of the bar next to a heavyset Bulgani miner. That was his first mistake. He tried to start a conversation with the Bulgani. That was his second mistake. Bulganis are not known as a social race. *You would not invite a Bulgani to a formal dinner party,* Jake thought. *He would be very unhappy, and you would be even unhappier.*

Jake and Nog were watching all this from the kiosk. They couldn't hear what the Fjori was saying, but Nog whispered to Jake that he knew what the Fjori was trying to do. Nog added, with a smile, that he had tried to do it himself more than once.

If there is one thing about the Fjori that earns them a grudging respect from the Ferengi, it is their ability to pull a con. Unfortunately, as Nog was about to observe, this particular Fjori, though full of youthful enthusiasm, lacked the professionalism of a true master of the art.

While Nog watched, anticipating what was about to come, Kala finally got the attention of the miner. Or, to be more exact, it was a trio of cloud crystals that Kala poured from a leather pouch onto the bar. Their beauty, and their value, was enough to attract the attention of even a hardened Bulgani miner.

"Ten strips of gold latinum," Kala said, naming his price.

The Bulgani grunted. "These are stolen."

"They are not. My grandfather gave them to me just before he died. They are family treasures."

"Then why do you sell them?"

"Because I must," Kala sighed. "I have a small sister to care for. She is sickly and I have no money for doctors." He touched the nearest of the three crystals. "These are all I have."

The Bulgani looked at the crystals while trying to hide his emotions. But Nog knew what he must be thinking: that they were worth much more than ten gold latinum, and he was certain that the Fjori had stolen them. For a moment he might have even considered calling the station security guards, but that moment passed quickly. If the Fjori had stolen them from someone else, then it was only right that he steal them from the Fjori.

"Five gold latinum," was the Bulgani's offer.

"You have me at a disadvantage," Kala whimpered. "You know I must sell them, so you attempt to cheat me."

The Bulgani lifted one of the crystals. The game was afoot. "Perhaps six latinum."

Kala snatched the crystal from the Bulgani's thick paw, then picked up the other two from the bar. He put all three back into their pouch and stood up as though he were going to leave. "I am sorry to have taken up your time."

The Bulgani was hooked. "All right. I have only eight latinum."

Kala hesitated. He began to put the pouch away. Hesitated again. Then he sat down and lay the pouch on the bar in front of the Bulgani. "Let me see your money."

The Bulgani took out a stack of shiny latinum strips and placed them on the bar next to the pouch. Kala counted them. Eight exactly. "I should not accept this, but I desperately need the money."

Kala stuffed the bars into his inner pocket. He started to push the crystals toward the Bulgani—but in the process he knocked over a glass of Bajoran sand beer.

The Bulgani instinctively jumped to avoid being splashed—and Kala seized the distraction to switch the bag on the bar with another that was hidden in his jacket. That was his third mistake.

Quark had seen the switch but considered it none of his business. If the Bulgani was that stupid, he de-

12

served to lose his money. Quark retreated to the far end of the bar.

However, a Bajoran shopkeeper, who had also witnessed the switch and who did consider it his business, stepped forward. He reasoned that if the Bulgani lost all his money, he would have none to spend in his own shop.

Kala began to leave, but the Bajoran grabbed him by the shoulder and reached into the Fjori's inner pocket and removed the other pouch.

Nog nudged Jake. "Come on. This is our opportunity."

Jake wasn't quite sure what Nog was talking about, but he followed his Ferengi friend—although he was certain Nog was going to lead them into trouble.

Which is just what he did.

The Bulgani became furious when he realized he had been cheated. He pulled Kala away from the Bajoran. It was clear that his immediate intent was to rip Kala apart piece by piece. It was also clear that most of the crowd in Quark's welcomed this bit of live entertainment.

But Kala, like most Fjori, had been in scrapes before. He yanked the Bulgani's money from his pocket and tossed the latinum strips into the crowd— where everyone scrambled to retrieve them.

The Bulgani, seeing his fortune being snatched up by greedy strangers, loosened his grip on Kala. "That's my money," he shouted as he plunged into the crowd.

Kala turned, grabbed the pouch that he knew contained the real crystals and dashed out the place—knocking Jake over in the process.

Now the station security guards arrived and began to restore order. The sad-but-wiser Bulgani miner was able to recover only half of his money.

Jake picked himself up and went out onto the Promenade. He found Nog waiting for him, wearing a broad smile. "What're you so happy about?" Jake wanted to know.

Nog led his friend to a dark corner, then revealed the cause of his happiness. Nog held the other pouch in his hand. He opened it and revealed three cloud crystals—the real ones.

"There isn't a Fjori alive who can outcon a Ferengi," he said proudly.

"You can't keep them, Nog."

Nog replaced the crystals in the pouch. "You're right. That would be stealing." He tossed the pouch to Jake. "We must return them—to the Fjori."

Which is how Jake found himself reluctantly crawling behind Nog through an air duct that led to the docking ring. He agreed with Nog that they had an obligation to return the cloud crystals. He did not agree that this was the way to go about it.

But as they peered through the grill into the dimly lit docking bay, it was a little late to turn back.

Jake looked over Nog's shoulder and saw that the docking bay was deserted, except for some activity near the airlock. There, he could see several Fjori men and women busily working on the *Orak*'s navigational computer module. They had removed the unit from the ship and linked it to the docking bay's diagnostic system for testing.

Nog saw the situation as a stroke of luck. If he could get over there without being seen, he might gain access to the navigational starcharts. In his pocket was a small data recorder he had borrowed from his uncle Quark's office.

Nog carefully removed the grill and pulled it inside the duct. The ease with which he accomplished the task informed Jake that his Ferengi friend had done this before.

Quietly, Nog slipped from the duct onto the docking bay, hiding himself behind some crates. He turned and waved for Jake to follow. Then the young Ferengi silently vanished into the shadows.

Jake lowered himself from the duct's opening onto the hard floor, wondering just how he had been talked into this. It was easy enough to blame it on Nog, but he knew that a con artist can really only con someone who wants to be conned. Jake had wanted to visit the Fjori ship, and Nog provided a convenient excuse.

Jake took a few cautious steps, trying to remain in the shadows, then stopped. He wasn't sure just what to do next. Walk up to the first Fjori he saw and introduce himself? *Well,* he asked himself, *why not?*

Jake touched the bulge in his pocket where he had

stashed the crystals. After all, he did have a reason to be here.

But before he could take another step, he felt something cold and sharp press against the back of his neck.

"Hold it right there, *gajo.*"

CHAPTER 3

Jake stood for what seemed an eternity, frozen in his tracks. The tip of something cold and sharp pressed into his skin at the base of his neck. Finally the voice behind him spoke again. "What're you doing here, *gajo?*"

"Ah—" Jake's throat was dry and he had trouble making the words come out. "We're just—ah, just returning something."

"What would you have that belongs to the Fjori?"

Jake began to reach into his pocket. The point pressed harder, almost breaking the skin. "Ouch! Hey! I'm only going to show you."

"Do it slowly."

Jake complied and very, very slowly removed the pouch. He held the pouch in his right hand so that whoever was behind him could see it.

"Open it," the voice commanded.

Carefully, so as not to upset his captor, Jake did as he was told. He opened the pouch and spilled the three cloud crystals into his left palm.

"Where did you get those?"

"Someone left them behind at Quark's. I was only returning them."

A hand reached out and quickly removed the crystals from Jake. "Why not keep them for yourself?"

"Because they don't belong to me. To keep them would be stealing."

"That's a stupid answer . . . but it has the ring of truth." The point was removed from Jake's neck. "You can turn around."

Jake slowly turned. He was not sure who he expected to see, except that it was not the person standing in front him holding the thin, silver blade.

"My name is Vija." She was his age, perhaps a year older or younger. It was hard to tell with girls. Her amber hair was cut short, as short as his own, and she was quite pleasant to look at. Not beautiful, like Dabo girls, but attractive like a fresh breeze on a warm summer afternoon. She wore one of the Fjori's loose-fitting tunics, but even so Jake could tell she was slim and athletic.

"You're a girl." The words came out before Jake could stop them. He was embarrassed that he had been terrified by a girl.

Vija held up the blade and smiled. "This is as deadly in my hands as it would be in the hands of any male Fjori. There is no shame in being afraid."

"I wasn't afraid," Jake started to protest, then stopped and admitted, "Yes. I was."

"I would have been afraid, too." Vija put the blade

back into its sheath beneath her tunic, then held up the cloud crystals. "Just how did you come by these?"

Jake quickly summarized the encounter in Quark's. He made an effort to leave out the switch by the young Fjori, but Vija understood the attempted con. "Kala. He should have known better. This could cause us a lot of trouble on the station."

Jake handed her the pouch and watched as she replaced the crystals. He noticed that her eyes were emerald-green. "I'll speak to my father. Explain that it was all a mistake."

"Your father?"

"He's Commander Sisko. He runs Deep Space Nine. I'm Jake Sisko." He held out his hand.

Vija took his hand in a firm grasp. "Glad to meet you, Jake Sisko. I am Captain Vardk's daughter." She stepped back and looked at him. "You are an important person here?"

Jake blushed. "Not really. I'm just a kid. Like you."

For a moment Jake saw a flash of anger in Vija's eyes, then it passed. "Never call a Fjori that. Even the youngest among us does not like to be referred to as a child."

"I'll remember that."

"I believe you will." She smiled, and Jake sensed that he had passed some sort of initiation and had been accepted.

Vija put the pouch with the crystals under her tunic. "Come. We will return these."

Suddenly Jake realized he had totally forgotten about Nog. Where had his friend disappeared?

"Intruder!" The shout came from the direction of the Fjori ship. Jake knew it had to be Nog. He turned and saw that Vija was already on her way to the source of the commotion.

Although this would be an opportune time to slip away, Jake knew he could not desert his friend, even as he realized that Nog's rash actions could get them both into deep trouble.

Jake arrived on the scene in time to see Nog squirming, his right ear held tightly by a Fjori engineer. Several other Fjori, attracted by the shout, had gathered in front of the diagnostic system. The young Fjori Jake had seen in Quark's, the one Vija called Kala, was not so gently removing something from Nog's hand.

"It's a palm-coder. The Ferengi was trying to steal our starmaps."

What Jake had feared had happened. Nog had been caught red-handed trying to download data from the Fjori navigational computer. He wasn't sure how his Ferengi friend was going to get out of this spot.

At that moment, Kala noticed Jake in the background and pointed at him. "There's another. Get him."

Two of the Ferengi stepped forward, but Vija quickly moved between them and Jake. "Stop. He's a friend."

"Friend?" Kala snarled. "He's not one of us. What's he doing here?"

Vija held out the pouch. "He was returning something that you lost."

Taken aback, Kala pulled out the pouch he had retrieved from Quark's and opened it to reveal worthless glass beads. Angrily he pointed at Jake. "He stole my crystals."

"Then why would he take the trouble to return them?" Vija replied.

"Good question."

Jake recognized the commanding voice of the *Orak*'s captain. Jrl Vardk emerged from the airlock into the docking bay, and the other Fjori stepped aside as he approached. He took both pouches from Kala, who did not protest, and examined their contents.

"The Fjori are mistrusted enough without your giving people another reason to suspect our intentions." Vardk placed the two pouches in his pocket. "I will return these when we are back in space."

"Yes, Captain." Kala meekly stepped out of the way as Vardk approached Jake.

"We meet again, young Sisko. I thank you for returning that which Kala—ah, misplaced."

"I was returning them, too." Nog seized the opportunity to break free of the Fjori who held him and rushed over to join Jake.

"He tried to steal our starmaps," the Fjori engineer insisted.

"That's right, Captain. He tried to link into our computer with this." Kala handed Nog's palm-coder to Vardk.

The captain gave the palm-coder to the engineer. "Did the boy access anything?"

The engineer turned on the palm-coder, made some adjustments to the controls. "I don't think so."

Vardk turned to Nog. "Is there anything important on that coder?"

Nog hesitated. Jake nudged him in the ribs. "Tell the truth, Nog."

"No, sir," Nog said.

Vardk turned to the engineer. "Erase the memory. Make certain that nothing can be retrieved."

"Aye, Captain. And then?"

"Then return it to the boy."

Kala started to say something, then thought better of it and shut up. But another of the Fjori, a grizzled man with steel-gray hair and a thin scar on his cheek, stepped forward. "If you please, sir?"

"What is it, Trax?"

"It's the Ferengi. He has seen the screens. He's an outsider and by Fjori law he must be judged."

"I didn't see anything," Nog protested.

"Probably true," said the engineer as he returned the palm-coder to Vardk, who gave it back to Nog.

"We can't chance it," Trax argued. "Fjori law is plain on this."

"Yes, it is." Vardk thought for a moment. "But we are in Bajoran territory and on a Federation-run space station. It seems we have something of a diplomatic problem here." Vardk ran his fingers through his thick beard, looked over at Jake and Nog, then came to a decision.

Less than two hours later a conference took place in Ops. Major Kira represented the Bajoran government and Commander Sisko spoke for the Federation. Odo was present in his role as Deep Space Nine's security chief.

Captain Vardk described the situation, while Jake and Nog stood in a corner of the commander's office next to Kala.

When he had finished, Vardk set a half bar of

gold-pressed latinum on the desk. "This should cover the losses of the Bulgani miner."

"You're being very generous, Captain Vardk," Sisko said.

Vardk looked over at Kala. "It will be taken out of Kala's share of the ship's earnings. A lesson that will, I hope, prove fruitful."

Jake happened to glance over at Kala in time to catch an icy stare directed at him and Nog. It was apparent that he blamed them for his troubles.

"What about these two?" Commander Sisko indicated Jake and Nog, and while he wasn't glaring at them like Kala, it was equally obvious that he was not pleased. Jake had seen that stern expression before, and knew that it spelled serious trouble.

"No real harm has been done," Vardk said. "I can understand the boys' curiosity."

"But Docking Bay Seven was placed off limits," Odo argued. "And they are both old enough to obey the rules."

"True," Sisko agreed. "Although Jake's intent was to return Kala's crystals, he should have left that to Odo. I will make certain that both he and Nog are properly disciplined."

Kira stood up and stretched. "That seems to settle matters."

"Yes," Sisko agreed.

Captain Vardk stood up. "Our repairs have been completed, and we shall be departing Deep Space Nine within the hour. There will be no further opportunity for incidents."

"I trust your next visit here will not require another diplomatic conference," Sisko said as he rose to shake hands with the Fjori captain. Then he looked over at Jake and Nog. "I want to see both of you in my quarters in thirty minutes."

"Yes, sir," Jake said. He nudged Nog. They left the room.

As they came outside into the main area of Ops, Kira stepped up beside them. "A word of caution," she whispered. Both Jake and Nog admired the Bajoran major, and any advice she gave them was well worth their attention. "The Fjori are a very secretive race. Captain Vardk is stretching things to let you two off so easily."

"I swear I didn't see their starmaps," Nog said, not adding that it wasn't because he hadn't tried.

"Maybe not, but the Fjori don't know that for sure. While they won't disobey their captain openly, I suggest that the two of you keep a very low profile until the *Orak* has left Deep Space Nine."

It was at that moment that Captain Vardk and Kala came out of Commander Sisko's office. The angry glance that Kala threw at Jake and Nog in passing made Major Kira's words ring particularly true.

There were not a lot of people on the Promenade anymore. Jake and Nog walked slowly, lingering in front of the shops as they made their way toward the habitat ring where the Siskos' apartment was located. Neither boy wanted to be late, but neither did they want to arrive for their punishment before the appointed time.

"What do you think he'll make us do?" Nog asked.

"Whatever it is, I guarantee that we won't like it," Jake answered. "It's bad enough that he's commander, but he'll feel he has to act like a father as well. That's when it gets really bad."

"You're his son. He'll probably go easier on you."

"It doesn't work that way with humans, Nog. The closer you're related to someone, the harder the punishment."

Nog began to say something about being glad to be a Ferengi, but the words caught suddenly in his throat. He pointed at something over Jake's right shoulder. "I think we've got trouble," is what he finally did say.

Jake started to turn, but Nog stopped him. "Don't turn around."

"What is it?"

"That Fjori with the scar." They were standing in front of a Bajoran fashion shop. Nog pointed at the holo-mirror in the center of the shop. "Just pretend you're looking at the clothes."

Jake moved into a position where he could look into the holo-mirror. At the edge of the image he saw the reflection of the Fjori called Trax and another man wearing Fjori dress. "I think they've been following us," Nog whispered.

"What do they want?"

"I don't think we want to know."

Jake saw that the mirror image of the two Fjori was

growing larger. They were approaching the boys. "I think they know we've seen them."

Nog grabbed Jake by the arm and pulled him toward one of the maintenance passageways. "We'll take a shortcut to your quarters."

Jake wasn't so sure. "Maybe we'd be better off taking the turbolift." But when he noticed that Trax and the other Fjori were now hurrying toward them, he changed his mind and followed Nog.

It was dim in the passageway. It was also isolated from the more frequently used sections of the station. Jake knew that if they were caught in here, there would be little chance of help from any passerby.

"Relax," Nog said as he ran ahead of Jake. "I know what I'm doing."

Jake hoped so. He looked behind him and saw the two Fjori men entering the passage behind them. Then, as the boys rounded a sharp corner, Jake's worst fears materialized in front of him. The passageway directly ahead of them was blocked by a locked gate. "Great shortcut," Jake said.

"Trust me," Nog replied as he went to the lock. He quickly keyed in a code, and instantly the gate slid open.

"My uncle Quark showed me this route. He has eighty-four shortcuts in case of emergencies." Nog squeezed through the gate as soon the opening was wide enough. Jake was right behind him.

With the sound of approaching footsteps growing louder, Nog keyed in a second code. The gate began to close. But it seemed to Jake that it was taking much too long. Then, just as Trax and the other man dashed around the corner, the gate slid shut and locked. They were safe, or would be as soon as they got to Jake's quarters.

Which took them only three minutes, as they were running all the way. Out of breath, Jake pressed his palm against the entry access. The door opened.

Jake and Nog stepped inside. It was dark in the Sisko quarters. "Lights," Jake commanded the computer.

Even as the lights started to blink on, Jake heard a deep throat being cleared behind him. "That won't be necessary. You boys won't be staying."

That voice was the last thing either of them would remember for a long time.

CHAPTER 4

It took longer than the thirty minutes he had scheduled for Commander Sisko to reach his quarters. A maintenance emergency had kept him in Ops for more than an hour. When Chief O'Brien finally tracked down the problem, it turned out to be a false alarm.

That was strange enough. Vandalism on Deep Space Nine was almost unknown. Not because some of the base's inhabitants were less apt to engage in practical jokes than other people, but because on a self-contained space station the chances of getting caught at it were much greater than planetside.

What was even stranger was that Jake and Nog were not waiting for him when he did arrive at his quarters. He wondered if, because he was late, Jake had gone back to Ops to find him. He touched his insignia comm badge. "Sisko to Major Kira. Are Jake and Nog in Ops?"

"No," Kira replied. "The boys aren't here."

Benjamin Sisko was becoming upset. Late or not,

Jake should have stayed here. But finding him would be easy enough, since the commander had given his son a junior version of the standard Starfleet insignia comm badge that contained Jake's personal code.

"Tell me where Jake is," Sisko ordered Kira.

There was a long moment, then Kira replied, "According to the computer, he's in your quarters."

"But that's—" Sisko had started to say "impossible," but at that moment he glanced down—and saw Jake's Starfleet insignia lying on the floor.

Sisko stooped to pick it up. Something was very wrong. Jake would not have left his insignia here, not of his own free will. Quickly, he thought through the possibilities.

"Major," Sisko barked into his comm badge. "I want you to stop the Fjori ship from leaving. I'm on my way to Docking Bay Seven. Notify Security Chief Odo to meet me—"

"Commander," Kira interrupted. "I can't stop the *Orak* from leaving."

"You have my authorization. I'll take full responsibility."

"No, you don't understand. The Fjori ship has already left Deep Space Nine." She paused, apparently checking the computer, then added, "It passed through the wormhole into Gamma Quadrant twenty minutes ago."

Sisko fingered Jake's insignia. He had a terrible feeling that he knew exactly where his son was.

* * *

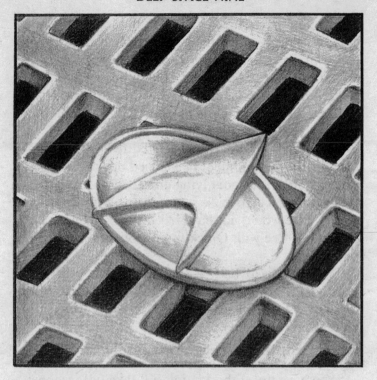

Which was more than Jake knew at that moment. Liquid blackness surrounded him. Jake felt as if he were swimming up through a dark ocean. His lungs were bursting. So far. It seemed he'd come so far, and there was still so far to go.

Suddenly, when he was convinced he'd never make it to the surface, there was light. Jake opened his eyes. He had been asleep and now he was awake.

But why had he been asleep? And where was he?

"We've been kidnapped." Nog was slowly rubbing his ears to restore their circulation.

"Someone was in our quarters." Jake was beginning to remember. There had been that voice behind him. Then he felt a cold mist. "That's the last thing I remember."

"Sensi sleep spray," Nog explained. "Quick and very effective. Uncle Quark keeps some behind the bar for emergencies."

"But where are we?" Jake looked around at his surroundings. There was a pale yellow glow that seemed to emanate from the ceiling. It was difficult to see, and he was still a bit dizzy. It took another minute to get his bearings.

"We're in some kind of storage closet," Jake said as he scanned the various crates that were held in place by magnetic straps. "We could be anywhere on the station."

"I think you better take a look outside." Nog pointed to a small viewport on the wall.

Jake stepped over and looked through the viewport. "This isn't the Bajor system. It's—"

"Gamma Quadrant," Nog finished. "We're on the other side of the wormhole."

"We really have been kidnapped. We must be on the *Orak*." For the first time, Jake noticed that the Starfleet insignia his father had given him was missing from his jacket. How would anyone ever find him? "Nog, we've got to get out of here!"

"Even if we could break out, it's a long walk back to Deep Space Nine."

Commander Sisko had convened an emergency meeting to decide what action to take. Odo confirmed what everyone there already knew. "Jake and Nog are not on the station."

"Which means?" Chief O'Brien asked.

"That they're on the *Orak*," replied Lieutenant Dax. "It's the only ship that's departed the station since the boys disappeared."

"So what do we do about it?" asked Dr. Bashir.

"Go after them, of course," said Kira.

Commander Sisko, who sat staring at the Operations Table during all of this, finally spoke. "No. We wait."

"Commander," Kira said, "Jake's your son. We have to go after him and Nog."

"Don't you think I want to do that?" Sisko snapped. "But how do we find the *Orak?* A single Fjori starship traveling in an unexplored quadrant. We wouldn't know where to begin a search."

Dax gently reached out and touched Sisko's hand. "Then what do you want us to do, Benjamin?"

"We have trading outposts in Gamma Quadrant. Some of them must have dealings with the Fjori. Start making contacts. Get me information."

"We're on it, Benjamin," Dax said as she and the others rose from the table.

"Odo," Sisko called after the station security chief, who stopped and looked back. "Talk to Quark. If anyone knows how to find the Fjori, it will be a Ferengi."

As the *Orak* continued on its journey, each unit of time taking it farther away from Deep Space Nine, Jake and Nog tried to understand their situation.

"Captain Vardk wouldn't have allowed this to happen." Jake was certain of that.

"He's a Fjori," Nog replied, as if that explained everything.

"Probably he doesn't know we've been kidnapped." Jake thought it was the only thing that made sense. "When we get to wherever we're going, then he'll send us back."

"Don't count on it. We'll be in Fjori space, and Fjori laws will apply. We could be in a real mess."

Jake started to say something, then thought better of it. It might have been Nog's fault that all this was happening to them, but this was not the time to start blaming one another. If they were ever going to get home again, they would have to work together.

Nog was seated in front of a black box in the corner. "Someone's given us a rather primitive replicator. At least they're not going to starve us."

"No, but it means we may be in here awhile." Jake looked out the viewport at the unfamiliar star patterns of Gamma Quadrant. "Wherever we're going, it's a long way from home."

CHAPTER 5

The *Orak* continued to fall like a silent stone through the long cold night of space. In the distance, one by one, the stars of Gamma Quadrant flickered out like candles in the wind.

Jake looked out through the small viewport. It seemed as though the *Orak* was being sucked into the maw of some gigantic black hole. Not only were they prisoners in the belly of this metal whale, but they were lost as well. For an instant Jake had a terrible feeling in his gut that he would never see Deep Space Nine or his father again.

Then, as he continued to stare into the black void between galaxies, he began to see it.

A tiny point of light.

Slowly, as he watched for what might have been only a few minutes or more than an hour, that point grew until it became a sun. A solitary sun. Like an island in a vast ocean of nothingness.

It was, Jake was certain, the sun that gave warmth

and life to the nameless world that the Fjori called their own.

Actually, as Jake would soon learn, the world did have a name. The Fjori called their world Ryft, which translated, roughly, to Eden. Which was an appropriate name, since this small planet on the edge of forever was like a garden in the middle of a great desert of black space.

Meanwhile, on another world, a metal one named Deep Space Nine, Security Chief Odo was visiting a place he would have described as a weed patch rather than a garden. He never understood the need for people to gather in cramped spaces, absorb unhealthy liquids, and play games that they were destined to lose.

Quark, on the other hand, understood it very well. It was how he made a very comfortable living. And he resented anything that interfered with the natural Ferengi pursuit of profit. "Of course I miss Nog." Quark considered his nephew an asset. Unlike Rom, Nog's father and Quark's brother, Nog was hardworking and smart.

"Then give me something to work with to find him," Odo said.

"The Fjori and Ferengi are not exactly the best of friends," Quark continued.

"Which is why you probably know more about them than any other race. Isn't it a Ferengi rule of acquisition to always know the competition?"

"Rule Number 218. But Ferengi don't consider the Fjori competition."

"Probably because the Fjori tend to bargain honestly."

"That is one of their weaknesses."

"I suppose in your view it is. But I am not here to discuss Ferengi philosophy. I want——"

"To find where the *Orak* has gone." Quark finished Odo's sentence. "Unfortunately, there is one secret that the Fjori are very good at keeping."

"And that is?"

"The location of the Fjori homeworld. That is the *Orak*'s destination."

And at that moment, light-years away from Alpha Quadrant, beyond even the traveled starpaths of Gamma Quadrant, the *Orak* neared Eden, a solitary planet spinning around a solitary sun.

"We're actually landing on the planet." Jake was amazed that the Fjori didn't use transporters to simply beam themselves down to the surface. "Landing a whole spaceship on a planet is—well, it's archaic."

"Archaic?" Nog asked.

"Means old-fashioned. Like cooking your meals instead of programming a replicator."

Nog glanced over at the crude replicator that had been their source of nourishment over the past three days. "They probably do that, too, judging from the condition of their replicators."

Jake looked out through the porthole at the landscape of the world. It appeared to be morning on this side of the planet, but a heavy gray mist made it hard to see what was out there. He turned and looked at the door. "Maybe they'll let us out of here now."

As if on cue, Jake heard the locking mechanism whir, and slowly the door slid open. There was a long moment of expectation and then the Fjori mate, Trax, came through the door.

"Last stop. This is where you get off," he said gruffly.

"You won't get away with this," Jake argued. "My father is commander of Deep Space Nine, a Starfleet officer, and—"

"And he has no idea where you are or where to start looking." Trax smiled with grim satisfaction. "You're on the planet Eden in Fjori territory. We make the rules here, not the Federation."

Trax looked at Jake and stepped forward, then stopped. "Where's the other one?"

Jake didn't know what he meant, until he looked around and saw that Nog was nowhere to be seen.

Trax's smile vanished and he raised his arm in a threatening manner. "Tell me where the Ferengi is."

"Right behind you."

Trax turned—just as the magnetic strips holding the cargo boxes were released and a dozen heavy crates broke free and tumbled onto him.

Nog, who had been hiding on the top of another group of boxes, leaped down and yelled at Jake, "Let's get out of here."

Jake looked over at Trax lying half buried under the pile of crates. Nog grabbed Jake's arm and pulled him toward the door. "He's going to have a real headache when he wakes up. Which is what we're going to have if we hang around until then."

Nog hurried through the door, and Jake was right behind him. They stepped into a narrow corridor.

"Which way?" Jake wondered. Then from one end of the corridor he heard heavy footsteps.

"Not that way." Nog spoke the obvious, and the two boys turned and ran in the opposite direction. They heard the footsteps pause, probably at the doorway of the cargo hold where they had been held prisoner, then there was some angry yelling and the footsteps began to run toward them.

This isn't good, Jake thought. *We're on an alien ship with no idea where to find the nearest exit.*

"Here," Nog whispered as if he were reading Jake's thoughts. Jake saw that his Ferengi friend had pulled out a small hatch cover and was squeezing through.

Jake was certain he could never fit through that opening, but somehow he did. Nog quickly pulled the hatch cover shut behind them. Then they sat stone still and held their breath as the footsteps approached and, without pausing, passed by their hiding place.

"That was close," Jake whispered as he breathed again.

"But now what do we do?" Nog wondered. "They'll alert the whole ship now that they know we've escaped."

"I don't think so," Jake said. He had been giving the

matter some thought, and it seemed to him that the fact they had been kept isolated in the cargo hold probably meant that Captain Vardk was unaware of the situation. He explained his theory to Nog.

"Then we have to find a way to get to him," Nog said, again stating the obvious.

"Easier said than done. They're going to have all the access routes to the control deck blocked. There's no way we'll sneak past."

"Not as long as we're *inside* the ship." Jake looked at Nog as the Ferengi finished his thought. "So we go *outside.*"

Which was, Jake thought, their only real choice. Inside the ship they were totally lost and easy prey. But outside they might have a chance. "But how do we get outside?"

"Hey," Nog replied, "this is a partnership. I told you what we have to do. It's your turn to figure out how to do it."

Jake thought about the problem. He had no idea of the layout of the Fjori ship. Even if they could get to a computer terminal without being seen, he didn't know the proper access codes. He wondered what his father would do in this situation. No, he interrupted himself, not his father. "O'Brien," he said aloud.

"O'Brien?"

"What would O'Brien do if he were in our place?"

"I don't understand." Nog was puzzled.

"This is an alien starship, but it needs to be serviced. These conduits will lead us to the outer shell of the ship. And somewhere in that outer shell there has to be an airlock or cargo doors."

Nog looked down the long dark conduit that stretched before them. "But this is a big ship. There must be miles of conduits. We could be lost in here for days."

Without bothering to reply, Jake started to crawl along the conduit. He was convinced this was the only chance they had. He was also convinced that if they didn't start moving, their kidnappers would soon figure out what they had done and be after them.

Nog, somewhat reluctantly, followed. Ferengi are not a race that enjoys crawling around in small dark places if it can be avoided.

Whenever they reached a branch, Jake would make an instant decision as to which route to take. Nog began to accept that his human friend might know what he was doing after all. Jake, on the other hand, was going on gut instinct and hoping that at least they weren't crawling around in circles.

After what seemed like hours they arrived at a cargo bay. "This is it," Jake whispered to Nog.

They looked through the grill and saw that most of the cargo had already been unloaded. That was bad, since they would have very little cover. Several Fjori were working in the area and would spot them before they reached the open cargo doors. Nog was willing to give the odds a try.

"No," Jake answered. "It's too far. They'd catch us. We need a diversion."

While he was trying to figure out what that might be, it came from an unexpected source.

"Break time." Jake peered through the grill and saw a Fjori entering the cargo hatch wheeling a food cart. The men paused in their work and ambled over to the cart. This was their chance—if they were fast enough.

Jake tried to remove the grill, but it was stuck. "I'm going to kick it free," he told Nog after several attempts that ended in failure. "The crew is at the other end of the cargo bay, so we'll only have a few seconds to get through the doors."

"Stop talking and start kicking," Nog replied impatiently.

Jake slid back, took aim, and struck at the grill with both feet. There was a loud clang, but the grill was still in place. He heard surprised voices. He kicked again. This time the grill broke loose and clattered as it hit the floor.

"What's that?" someone yelled.

Jake scrambled through the opening. Nog was so close behind that he tripped over Jake's feet as he hit the deck.

"Intruders! Grab them!"

Jake pulled Nog to his feet and they ran. Half a dozen burly Fjori crewmen were now racing to catch them.

It was close, but Jake and Nog managed to reach the open cargo doors ahead of their pursuers, and, without a thought as to what lay beyond, leaped through the opening into the wet, gray mist.

They landed on hard ground and rolled with the

impact. Unloaded cargo crates were stacked all around the area. Quickly Jake and Nog crawled behind one of the stacks as the men from inside the ship came out and looked around.

They could hear the men arguing about which way to search. Fortunately, the morning mist was still thick enough to provide cover.

Finally, they reached the perimeter of the landing area. The mist was burning off by now and they needed to find someplace safe to hide while they figured out their next move.

"Jake."

He froze. It was Vija's voice. He turned and looked up and saw her standing in front of him, silhouetted against the blood-red sun that was shining through the vanishing mist. "What are you doing here?"

Before he could reply, a large dark shadow stepped in front of her and blotted out the sun. Jake squinted and recognized Captain Vardk. "That's what I'd like to know."

CHAPTER 6

My daughter asked what you're doing here, Jake. I'd like to know the answer to that as well." Vardk towered over the two boys like a giant. But he was curious, not angry—not yet.

Vija came over to join them. Before Jake could explain, the crew that had been pursing them now appeared from all directions and surrounded them. One of them pointed at Jake and Nog. "They were hiding in the cargo bay."

"Stowaways," added another. They moved toward Jake and Nog, but Vardk raised an arm and they stopped.

"You were stowaways?" Captain Vardk asked Jake, obviously finding it difficult to believe.

"Not exactly," Jake replied, brushing the wet soil from his jacket. "We were—"

"Kidnapped," Nog interrupted.

"Kidnapped? By who?"

"By us, Captain." Trax emerged from behind a stack of crates. Following him were several Fjori, including the youth Kala, who stared at Jake with obvious malice.

"Why, Trax?" demanded Vardk. "These lads are citizens of the Federation. You've broken the law."

"No, Captain. With all due respect, it was *you* who broke Fjori law when you let them go back on Deep Space Nine."

Vardk turned on Trax and his comrades and seemed about to explode with pent-up anger, then his stances softened, but his look and his voice were still hard as Klingon steel. "I'll decide your punishment later, Trax. For now I want a scout ship ready to return these two through the wormhole within the hour."

"We can't do that, Captain." Trax paused, then continued before Vardk could respond. "You no longer have the authority to order us."

Jake leaned over to Vija. "What's he talking about? Your father's the captain. He's in command."

"That's true in space," Vija said. "But when you stepped onto the planet's surface, the captain is no longer the supreme authority that he is on the ship."

"They wanted us to escape," Nog realized. "It's the kind of trick a Ferengi would play." Frightened as he was, there was a hint of admiration in his voice.

Trax walked over to Jake and Nog. He pointed at them while he addressed his words to the captain. "They have broken Fjori law. And by Fjori law, they must be punished."

"That is not for you to decide, Trax."

"No, Captain. But neither is it your decision to make." Trax looked beyond the captain into the faces

of the Fjori who had gathered to see what all the commotion was about. "I demand trial by council."

Captain Vardk looked at Trax and his fellows for a long moment, then the hardness in his face vanished into resignation. "That is your right, Trax. I will call upon the Council of Elders to decide this at first light on the morrow."

"We will abide by their rule," Trax said. "Until then we leave the offworlders in your custody."

Trax walked away and his companions followed. Kala lingered for a moment. He stared at Jake and seemed about to say something, then glanced at Vija and held his tongue, turned and left. Slowly, like leaves carried away by the wind, the rest of the Fjori departed. Finally there was only Jake, Nog, Captain Vardk, and Vija.

"Find Jake and Nog a place to stay," Vardk told Vija. "Explain to them about our ways so that they can understand what is happening." Then he looked at Jake. "With your permission, young Sisko, I will speak for you at tomorrow's trial."

"Thank you," Jake replied. "Nog and I accept."

Vardk nodded, then walked away toward the ship.

"What can I do for you, Jake?" Vija asked when her father was gone.

"One thing," Jake replied. "Tell me how Nog and I can get home."

Halfway across the galaxy, sitting alone in his darkened quarters, Benjamin Sisko was having a similar thought. So lost in his thoughts was he that the door buzzed three times before he heard it.

"Enter."

The door slid open and Jadzia Dax, the Trill Science Officer who had been Sisko's good friend through two human hosts, came inside. She looked over at the table and the untouched evening meal. "You need to eat something."

"I wasn't hungry."

"Yes, you were, or you wouldn't have ordered from the replicator." She looked closer. "Two settings?"

"Force of habit, I guess."

She sat down next to Sisko and gently touched his hand. "I want him back, too, Benjamin. Almost as much as you do."

"It's just that I—feel so helpless, Dax." He looked into her eyes and the wisdom from numerous lifetimes they contained, and was grateful that there was one person on Deep Space Nine with whom he could drop his role of commander and just be himself. "My son's been taken from me." He tried to put his troubled thoughts into words. "And there's nothing I can do to get him back."

"You're doing what you can, Benjamin. That's all you can do."

"Maybe I should be out there in Gamma Quadrant —searching."

"You know that's nonsense. That's a huge ocean out there, and you'd be looking for a rowboat. Finding it would be a miracle."

"But at least I'd be doing something more than putting out diplomatic inquiries. I'm tossing bottles into the sea and hoping they make it to the opposite shore."

"Perhaps they will. And remember that there's someone out there who is doing what you would do because that's how you've taught him." She looked at him with quiet reassurance as she added, "Trust Jake to find a way home again."

* * *

49

It was sunset on the planet Eden. Jake sat with Vija and Nog on a small bluff that overlooked the sprawling village. Eden was a desert world, and the twilight air was cool and sweet as the native cactus flowers released their fragrance. It was, Jake thought, quite a beautiful world, and reminded him of the high country of New Mexico on Earth where his father had once taken him camping.

Below them the rambling village of sandstone huts appeared almost medieval. The houses clustered along an ambling river that cut a wide green swath through the red-brown earth. Like the planet, the village was an oasis in the midst of a harsh landscape.

"This is were you grew up?" Jake asked Vija.

"No. I was born on the *Orak*. That is my world. Eden is only the place where the Fjori gather. The ship is my home. For the Fjori, our ships are our only real home."

"But someone lives here," Nog said.

Vija smiled. "The elders and those who are assigned to work here."

Jake looked out at the spaceport that spread across a dry lake beyond the village. Besides the *Orak*, there were five other starships reflecting the light of the amber sky. "How many Fjori are there?"

"I don't know if even Great-Grandmother knows the answer to that. We are the Fjori, our families are scattered across the starways like grains carried by the starstreams."

Nog pointed at the starships docked into landing grids on the planet's surface, a sight he was unaccustomed to seeing. "Don't you have transporters on your ships?"

Vija laughed. "Of course we do. But this is Eden. Here we use the old ways, even when it comes to unloading cargo. It may not be as efficient, but it is our tradition."

"And what does your tradition say will happen to us?" Jake asked.

For a long moment Vija was silent. "Once a very long time ago there was another planet that was also called Eden. It, too, was the home of the Fjori. But an outsider discovered the secret location of that Eden. A great space armada came and demanded the treasure that was rumored to be hidden there. But there was no treasure."

"What happened?"

"They took out their anger on Eden for denying them what we did not have. Every building on the planet was destroyed. Those of the families that were not murdered were sold into slavery."

Vija lowered her head. The incident she spoke of had happened long before she was born, long before any Fjori now living had been born. It was only a distant memory but it clearly still burned bright in the consciousness of every Fjori.

"Less than a hundred of our ships escaped. In the centuries since, we have rebuilt the fleet." Vija looked at Jake, her eyes cold as Rjoran ice. "But the Fjori have never forgotten. We have vowed that no one who is not of the family can ever be in a position to reveal the secret of this Eden."

"Does that mean what I think it does?" asked Nog.

"It means that under Fjori law, neither of you can ever leave Eden."

The next morning as the first light from the blood-red sun that warmed Eden broke over the peaks of the distant blue mountains, Jake and Nog emerged from the hut where they had spent a restless night. There were no guards, and Nog suggested that they try to escape. Jake replied that the reason the Fjori didn't need to guard them was that there was nowhere for them to run. Beyond the quiet tranquility of the village, there was only burning desert and hostile mountains.

"We wouldn't have a chance out there," Jake concluded. Nog had to nod in agreement.

As Vija led them to the place where their trial would take place, Jake noticed that the Fjori they passed were neither friendly nor unfriendly. In fact they ignored the two offworlders as though they did not exist.

"You are *gajo* in their eyes," Vija explained.

"What exactly does *gajo* mean?" Jake asked.

"It means that you are considered something not quite human. The Fjori treat all outsiders as *gajo,* as someone not worthy."

"That attitude's not going to earn you a lot of friends."

"No. The Fjori have learned over the years not to trust anyone. We have been betrayed too often."

"But until you learn to have trust in something, the Fjori are always going to be isolated."

Vija looked at Jake. "You are right. And there are those among us, mostly the young, who believe it may be time for the Fjori to reach out to other races."

Their conversation was interrupted as they reached their destination at the edge of the village, where a large open amphitheater cut into the hard ground.

Jake saw a group of people he assumed to be the Council of Elders sitting silently in a semicircle in the center of the arena as Vija ushered them down the steps. He noticed only about two dozen Fjori seated around the perimeter. "We don't seem to be attracting too much attention," Jake commented.

"There is no reason for them to be curious. Fjori law is very clear on this situation," Vija said. "The verdict is certain."

"Then why bother with a trial?" asked Nog.

"Tradition," answered Vija. "Besides, Great-Grandmother is head of the council. She is wise and may find a way for you to return home." Vija's eyes scanned the members of the council. "Except that she is not here."

"Grandmother is on retreat." Captain Vardk joined them as they approached the council. "We will not have the advantage of her wisdom on the council this day."

That doesn't sound like a very good beginning, Jake thought to himself.

* * *

A short time later Jake's unspoken prophecy came true. Even with Captain Vardk arguing that their "crime" was one of youth and misjudgment, there was no appeal from the rigid rules of the Fjori. The six members of the Council of Elders listened to the facts and made their decision after only a few minutes of hushed deliberation.

Jake was not surprised that neither he nor Nog were asked to testify. Apparently what a *gajo* had to say, even on his own behalf, was considered irrelevant.

"It has been decided," the leader of the council said, "that the two offworlders have violated Fjori laws and must serve the appropriate sentence. They will remain on this planet for the rest of their natural lives. By the steel of the ship and the fire of the planet, I declare this council closed." As one body the six council members stood and prepared to make their exit.

Captain Vardk put his hand on Jake's shoulder and whispered in his ear, "I'm sorry, Jake. I was afraid it would turn out like this."

"Isn't there any way you can contact my father?" Jake asked. "He'd know what to do."

"The law forbids me to do that." Vardk lowered his head. "It may not be right or just, but it is our way. It is our law."

Jake glanced over to the side of the arena and saw the Fjori youth, Kala, smiling at him. It was a taunting smile, and Jake was certain that Kala would do everything in his power to make sure that Jake and Nog did not enjoy their stay on Eden.

1995

"If only Great-Grandmother were here," Vija said. "She might have found a way."

"Perhaps she would," Vardk agreed. "But she is not scheduled to return from retreat for another six moons. By then the council's decision will be final and there can be no arguments."

"You mean," Jake interrupted, "the decision isn't final yet?"

"It requires three full moons before any decision is closed. During that time the defendants can still argue for another finding."

"Then let's argue," said Nog, the gears in his Ferengi mind already grinding.

"I'm sorry, Nog," Vardk said. "You are *gajo* and cannot argue before the council."

Nog's oversized ears appeared to droop at the captain's statement. He knew every Ferengi rule of acquisition by heart, and yet there would be no opportunity to use them. It wasn't fair.

"It isn't fair." Vija's words echoed Nog's unspoken thought. Suddenly she rose and intercepted the council, who were about to leave the arena.

"Wise elders," she called to them. "I speak as the Fjori voice of those who have no voice." She pointed at Jake and Nog. "I would demand that these two have the right to cleanse themselves of their misdeeds through the Rite of Passage."

CHAPTER 7

No!" The yell came from Kala, who was standing near the exit and heard Vija's words. He ran forward. "They are not Fjori. They cannot take the Rite of Passage."

"It is not forbidden," argued Vija.

The leader of the council thought about this for almost a minute before he answered. "No. It is seldom done, but it is not against our law."

Kala seemed to want to shout in angry protest, yet he remained dutifully silent in the presence of the council.

The council elder walked over to where Jake and Nog stood next to Vardk. His first words were to the captain. "Your daughter pleads that these two take the Fjori Rite of Passage. Are they worthy?"

Without hesitation, Vardk replied, "They are worthy."

"And how are they worthy?" the elder inquired.

"In their own space both are princes. Jake is the son of the commander of the guardian of the wormhole

57

they call Deep Space Nine." *That's pretty close to the truth,* Jake thought.

"Nog is the heir to the great Ferengi trading empire of Quark." That was a bit more of a stretch, but it had enough truth to be acceptable.

"I trust your words, Vardk. Your grandmother is our eldest, and you are an honorable man." The elder turned to Jake and Nog. "Do you accept trial by Rite of Passage?"

Jake looked at Nog. Whatever this Rite of Passage was, it might be their only way to ever getting home again. "We accept," they replied in unison.

"Then let it be done." The elder looked up at the sky and pointed. "When the sun reaches its zenith, your Rite of Passage will begin." He turned away.

When the elder was gone, Jake asked Vardk, "Just what is this Rite of Passage?"

"It is the ritual that every young Fjori must pass in order to leave the protection of childhood and take on the responsibilities of an adult. From the moment of our birth each of us prepares for the ordeal."

"Ordeal?" asked Nog. He didn't like the sound of that word. Ferengis much prefer pleasure to the possibility of pain.

"It won't be so bad," Vija said as she joined them.

"I wish that were true, daughter. But these two are outsiders who have had no preparation for the struggle that awaits them."

"If we pass this Rite of Passage, what then?" Jake asked.

"Then, young Sisko, you will be received into the Fjori family. You would no longer be offworlders."

"And we can go home again?"

Vardk nodded. "I believe the council might then consider it."

"Great."

"Perhaps," Vardk said in a solemn voice. "My daughter has given you an opportunity to gain your freedom, but the Rite of Passage for someone inexperienced in our ways is dangerous at best. It may be an opportunity you will have wished you had not accepted."

They had less than three hours to prepare for their opportunity. To begin with, Vija explained to them the rules of the Fjori Rite of Passage.

It's really very simple, Jake thought when she had finished. He and Nog would leave the village at noon, cross the desert and go into the mountains to retrieve a feather from the Graf, some kind of bird that lived in the high peaks.

"Not exactly a bird," Vija interrupted. "More like a flying snake."

"Sounds like something I wouldn't like to meet," Nog said. Ferengis had a strong dislike for anything that slithered, and something that slithered and flew was even more to be avoided.

"We can handle it," Jake assured his friend.

"You handle it. I'll watch."

"Your real trouble will come from the chasers. Six

men will start in pursuit of you two hours after you leave the village. If they catch you before you retrieve the feather and return here, you fail."

"How much time do we have?" Jake asked.

"This day and two more. You must be back before the sun sets on the third day."

"We can do it," Jake announced loudly. He only wished he felt as much bravery as he expressed.

Vija spent the rest of their preparation time showing them holographic maps of the region surrounding the village. Jake picked out three of the most obvious routes to the mountains, then discarded them. Their chasers would know those routes and, being more experienced in the ways of this planet, would probably catch them.

"We need a more difficult route that causes as many problems for our chasers as it does for us."

Nog looked at the maps. Finding the most devious path to a destination was something a Ferengi did naturally. After a moment he ran his finger through the hologram and traced out a winding route. "This is how we should go."

"It is a good choice," Vija said.

Nog smiled. "This is going to be fun."

"No," Jake contradicted him. "Not fun. This is going to be difficult and dangerous." He paused, then added, "But if we work together as a team, we can do it—and get home again."

High noon on the planet arrived a lot sooner than Jake would have liked. By then, having had time to reflect, he had lost a great deal of his original confidence. Eden, in spite of its name, was a harsh and hostile environment. There were unknown creatures lurking out there in addition to the Graf, which would pose dangers to two unsuspecting boys.

Yet here he was, standing at the edge of the village, waiting to confront those dangers. In a game, or in a battle, there is always that moment before it starts when you begin to doubt. The elder Sisko had confided that to his son the time Jake faced an overwhelming Klingon foe during a Starfleet Youth Olympics when they were living on Mars. It was only supposed to be a game, but Klingons take even their games with deadly seriousness.

Jake had been afraid, but he was even more afraid to admit to his fear. Benjamin Sisko had sensed his son's apprehension and explained that it was not something to be ashamed of, that it happened to everyone. Fear was natural, and the real test of courage was not in denying your fear, but in accepting it and moving through the fear. Jake did and, to his surprise, won the match.

Jake remembered that moment with pride now as he took a deep breath, forced a smile for Vija and her father, and stared out at the desert and mountains beyond, glistening in the warm sun. Then, shielding his eyes, he looked up at the sky with the sun nearing its zenith. He had been relieved when Vija told them this was autumn on the planet and they wouldn't have to confront the terrible heat of Eden's summer.

He flashed a grin at Nog, standing next to him. They

had both been given loose-fitting Fjori tunics, as well as boots of soft fur on the inside and a reptilian leather on the outside that were sturdy enough to climb over a field of Orgonian razor rocks. They each carried a single water container, enough to last one full day. When it was gone, they would have to search out their own source, but the filtering cup on the container would purify any liquid. "It might taste sour," Vija had explained as she demonstrated how the filter worked, "but it will quench your thirst." She had also told them the best places to find water.

Nog wanted weapons for protection but was told politely but firmly that weapons of any sort were forbidden.

"For a good reason," Vardk explained. "With a weapon you will feel inclined to fight rather than flee. While running from danger may not be the mark of a hero, it is that of a survivor. The Rite of Passage is a test of survival."

"Does everyone succeed?" Jake asked.

"Not everyone." There was a laugh, and Jake turned to see Kala. "And certainly not you."

The Fjori youth was to be one of their chasers. Jake was not surprised, but he wasn't sure why Kala seemed to hate him so much.

"It's Vija," Nog whispered to Jake as they stepped apart from the others, counting down the last minutes until the ritual began.

"Vija?" Jake hadn't realized he had been voicing his thoughts aloud, either that or his Ferengi friend was telepathic.

"How can you be so dense, even for a human?" Nog wondered. "It's obvious that Kala likes Vija, and you put him down in front of her. She likes you. Kala's jealous and wants to get even any way he can."

Jake looked back at Kala, and the angry glare that stared back at him more than confirmed Nog's words. Kala had a personal stake in seeing them fail, and Jake realized that the Fjori would do anything in his power to make sure that he and Nog did not survive. The thought gave him a queasy feeling in the pit of his stomach like a meal of overripe gzzo beans.

"Let the Rite of Passage begin." The council elder's voice was loud and clear as he raised his arm and then let it fall to his side.

Jake and Nog hesitated, not quite sure what they were expected to do next. "Go," Vija yelled at them.

And suddenly they were off—running away from the oasis of the village into the hostile planet and to whatever unknown perils awaited them out there.

CHAPTER 8

They were a thousand meters from the village and running at top speed when Nog tugged at Jake's tunic. "We have a long way to go."

Jake slowed to a fast trot. Nog was right. Running as fast as they could, they would be exhausted before they were halfway across the desert.

The ground beneath their feet was firm, and they made good progress as the village behind them vanished below the horizon. Jake continued to set their pace, fast enough to ensure they would have a good lead by the time the chasers came after them, but not so fast that they'd drop from exhaustion and become easy quarry.

Adrenaline rushed through his veins. Jake felt early runner's exhilaration at the start of a race, knowing that each step carried them closer to going home again. Nothing was going to stop them.

They were an hour away from the village when the ground started to turn soft. It was like wading through water, and their pace slowed dramatically. This reminded Jake of the Great Red Desert on Mars, where his father had taken him for a weekend camping trip.

"Don't run," Jake cautioned Nog. "We won't get there any faster, and we'll just use up all our energy."

They stopped trying to run and walked, which made it easier to move through the soft sand. "They'll catch up with us if we don't hurry." Nog worried.

Jake shook his head. "No. They'll have the same problem with the sand as we do. As long as we keep moving at a steady pace we'll be okay."

They were twenty minutes into the sand when they could see the hard ground again in the distance. Jake recognized it as the rock canyon that led into the mountains.

"What's that?"

Jake looked to where Nog was pointing and saw what appeared to be a small sand hill that lay directly in their path. He said as much, then slowed as they approached the obstacle. He was trying to remember something Vija had said during the morning. She had given them so much information that their brains had been on overload. Much of what she said had been forgotten.

They were almost to the hill when a spurt of sand erupted from its center. Suddenly Jake remembered what Vija had told them. "Sand Seeker," he yelled at Nog, who was several steps ahead of him.

Nog stopped dead in his tracks. Not because of Jake's warning—but because *something* was emerging from the middle of the hill.

It reminded Jake of one of the Bajoran tubular bugs

that the boys had learned about at school back on Deep Space Nine. But this bug was a lot bigger, almost twice their size. The Sand Seeker's mouth seemed gigantic as it opened up, and the only thing Jake could think of was that they were about to be swallowed by a sand whale.

"Nog! Run!" Jake shouted, but it was unnecessary, as his Ferengi friend had already turned and was heading away from the hill—with the creature in relentless pursuit.

Nog stumbled and pitched forward. Jake, without breaking his pace, grabbed hold of Nog by the nearest handle—his oversized ear—and pulled him to his feet.

Behind them the Sand Seeker slid effortlessly through the sand like a power sled. It was in its natural environment, and Jake realized there was no way they were going to outrun the creature.

"Up there," he shouted at Nog.

With the Sand Seeker's open maw snapping at their heels, the boys took three giant strides and leaped up onto an outcropping of rock that jutted out of the sand.

It was only the size of a tabletop and rose less than two meters from the surrounding ground, but it was a tiny island of safety in the dangerous sea of sand. The Sand Seeker had no arms or legs and could not maneuver up the rigid rock surface.

"Did you have to pull so hard on my ear?" Nog asked when they had time to catch their breath.

"Hey, you're safe," Jake replied.

Rubbing his sore ear, Nog had to admit that his human friend probably saved his life. He looked down at the sand and saw the creature burrow back beneath the surface. "Let's move."

"No," Jake said. Nog had started to climb down off the rock, when the Sand Seeker spurted its sand warning and reemerged from where it had been waiting. Nog leaped back up onto their rock table sanctuary.

"That thing's not stupid," Jake said. "It's going to try and wait us out. So we'll just have to outwait it."

"We can't," Nog argued. He looked back across the desert in the direction they had come. "Kala and the others are going to be after us by now. They'll catch us if we don't keep moving."

Jake realized that Nog was right. They couldn't stay here on this protective rock for very long. He looked down at the sand, certain the creature was waiting for them just below the surface, and recalled an old Terran phrase his father had once used. "We're caught between a rock and a hard place."

Which was precisely how, many light-years away on Deep Space Nine, Commander Benjamin Sisko felt as he sat alone in his office in Operations in front of an unresponsive computer screen.

It was that quiet time when the rush of the day's activities was past, when there were no particular diplomatic crises to referee or technological glitches created by obsolete Cardassian hardware to oversee. At the moment he had nothing to occupy his mind except the gnawing worry that his son was lost and alone somewhere out there beyond the wormhole, and he was beginning to doubt whether he would ever see him again.

There was a muffled cough, and Sisko looked up from the computer to see Quark standing in the doorway. "If you're busy, Commander," he apologized for the interruption.

"No. Please come in."

"I was wondering—actually, Rom was asking me —if there was any word about Jake or Nog?"

"Nothing, I'm afraid." Sisko gestured for Quark to sit, and the Ferengi seated himself in one of the standard issue chairs. "I'm so anxious about Jake, I'd forgotten that you must be terribly concerned as well," Sisko apologized.

"I like the boy, and I'd miss a good hard worker in my establishment." Quark reached over to a tray on the commander's desk and poured himself a glass of what he imagined to be Starfleet private label synthehol, but which turned out to be Bajoran mineral water. "It's Rom that particularly worries me. He hardly ever seemed to pay any attention to Nog, but now he's beside himself with grief—and his mistakes are costing me a fortune."

Sisko listened quietly while Quark put on his usual hard-eared calculating Ferengi front, but the commander could sense that there was a real concern underneath the words. Finally, Quark leaned across the desk. "Commander, you have to do something. You have to get Nog back—and Jake, too."

"We're doing everything we can," Sisko replied, but in the back of his mind he wondered if that was true. Deep Space Nine probes had made contact with other Fjori ships, but they of course had refused to get involved and would offer not even a hint of where their secret homeworld was located. In fact, they all denied that such a planet even existed.

Security Chief Odo suggested that he might be able to infiltrate one of the Fjori ships disguised as a piece of Jjvania ceramic to gain information, but Sisko could not condone breaking Federation laws—even if the fate of his own son might hang in the balance.

No, he thought, *there must be another way.* But he had no idea what it was. "Care for another drink?" he asked Quark.

The Ferengi forced himself to finish off the mineral water and started to shake his head, but Sisko opened a drawer and pulled out a bottle of rare Vulcan ale. "Ah, perhaps just one more."

For a long time the two of them sat in the office and drank the warm green liquid and talked about how much trouble Jake and Nog had created with some of their adolescent antics. "I really miss them, Commander," Quark said as he recalled how they almost ruined his place with a Ventazan Volcano Sundae.

"So do I," Sisko said quietly. Then he recalled what Dax had said to him and repeated it to Quark. "Trust them to find a way home again."

At the moment, Jake's immediate concern was finding a way past the creature that circled like a hungry shark just beneath the sand surrounding their tiny rock sanctuary. Nog was right that they had to keep moving or Kala and the other chasers would catch up to them. But how to get by the Sand Seeker?

"It's not that far to hard ground." Nog pointed to where the sand ended and the rocky ground began less than two hundred meters away.

Jake thought about it, then looked at the soft sand they would have to go through. There was no way they could outrun the creature—unless they had a diversion. Jake wondered what they might use as he went over their meager inventory in his mind.

He reached under his tunic and took out the Fjori water container. Just maybe it would work. He unscrewed the filter top. "What're you doing?" Nog asked.

"Water," Jake explained. "That's what Vija told us the Sand Seeker is after."

"But we'll need all the water we have," Nog protested.

"It's not going to do us any good if we don't get away from here pretty quick."

Nog thought about their options. He hated to give up half their water supply, but they had no choice. "So what's the plan?" he asked.

"I'm going to throw this as far as I can." Jake held the container upright so as not to spill any of the water. "Then we're going to jump and run—as fast as we can."

"Suppose the Sand Seeker doesn't go for the water container?"

"Then we may have a problem." Jake tried to sound flip, but his stomach was churning as he prepared to throw the container. "Ready?" he asked Nog.

"Go for it," Nog replied as he gave a thumbs up.

Recalling his father's baseball tips in Deep Space Nine's holosuite, Jake took a windup and then tossed the container as though he was throwing a baseball from right field to home plate.

The container traveled through the air in a high arc, water spilling as it spun, then landed with a soft thud on the sand about twenty meters away.

Without waiting to see if the Sand Seeker took the bait, Jake and Nog leaped off the other side of the rock. Half expecting the monstrous creature to rise out of the sand in front of them, Jake hesitated for a moment—then ran after Nog, who was already sprinting through the sand.

Jake felt as if he were running in slow motion, with each step becoming harder than the one before. It seemed he wasn't making any progress, and he was tempted to glance back over his shoulder but knew better. That would only waste energy, and energy was something he couldn't afford to waste.

His lungs bursting, Jake caught up with Nog, who had a three-step head start on him, and together, stride for stride, they ran toward the hard ground. Certain he could feel the sand shifting behind him as the Sand Seeker torpedoed toward them, Jake pushed himself even harder.

It seemed he had been running forever when his feet

hit stone. He stumbled but kept running. After a dozen more steps he collapsed onto the hard earth.

Gasping for breath, Nog tumbled on top of him. For a long time they lay there, breathing hard and sweating from their effort, listening to the Seeker slide away in defeat.

Finally Jake rolled over and sat up. He saw they were safe. The desert was behind him and they were into the canyon country that led to the mountains.

His throat was dry, and he turned to Nog. "Let me have a sip of your water."

Nog reached under his tunic and his hand came out empty. "It's gone." He looked out at the sand. "I must have dropped it when we were running."

"No," Jake said, not wanting to believe that they had lost both of their water containers. "Now what're we going to do?"

CHAPTER 9

What they did was continue on their quest. Moving into rocky, low canyon country, their progress was slow, and the shadows of late afternoon continued to lengthen. It was becoming more and more difficult to see what was ahead. The lack of water was not helping matters.

"I'm getting thirsty," Nog complained.

"Don't think about it," Jake replied. "It will only make you thirstier." His own mouth was dry and he would have given anything for a tall cold glass of Kilarian kola.

"It's getting dark," Nog said, changing the subject.

Jake looked up at the canyon rim. The sun was out of sight now over the edge. It would be another hour or two before the actual sunset, but the light from the sun didn't reach far into the canyon.

"We need to find shelter while we can still see something," Jake realized. The last thing he wanted was to be wandering around here in darkness. They might stumble into Kala and the chasers—or something a whole lot worse.

Nog scanned the horizon, which seemed to be all rock and stone. They might find a big boulder and huddle behind it, but the idea didn't excite him. They needed something like—

"There!" Nog stopped so abruptly that Jake, who was following close behind, nearly stumbled.

"Nog, warn me next time you're going to do that."

Ignoring Jake's complaint, Nog pointed up at a dark spot thirty meters above them. "See," he urged Jake. "It's a cave."

Jake looked but did not quite see. Ferengis have better night vision than humans, so Jake had to assume that Nog was right. It was a cave. Or, at least, he hoped it was a cave.

"How do we get to it?" Jake looked at the canyon wall, which seemed to rise straight up. There wasn't a trail that he could see, and climbing in this twilight dark wasn't a good idea. He said as much to Nog.

"No. We don't climb up. We climb *down*."

Jake was totally confused, until he saw what Nog had seen. Off to the left was the dry bed of what had been a small waterfall eons ago, when Eden was a wet planet. Centuries of dripping water had worn away the canyon wall, leaving almost a stairway. Then, some distance above the dark spot, there was a ledge that led directly over the mouth of the cave. Or what Jake hoped was a cave.

"We get up there and we won't be able to get back down in the dark," Jake told Nog.

"Got a better idea?"

Jake didn't, so they started climbing.

The first few meters were easy, but it soon became more difficult. The canyon rock was dry and brittle. It broke away if they weren't careful. They had to take the climb slowly and cautiously. A fall would certainly result in a broken leg, if they were that lucky.

By the time Jake and Nog reached the ledge, it was nearly dark. The sky above the canyon was streaked with red from the dying sun. It was also getting chilly. Vija had told them the nights on Eden could be quite cold. That was another reason they needed to find shelter as soon as possible.

The rocky ledge was very narrow, just wide enough to walk along if they leaned in against the canyon wall. Nog continued to take the lead. Jake followed, wishing he could see better. On the other hand, with the bottom of the canyon a long way beneath them, maybe it was better that he couldn't see all that well.

"Watch the loose rock," Nog cautioned.

Jake's foot hit a stone and it tumbled noisily down the canyon wall. "I see what you mean."

"Oops." Nog stopped short.

"What oops?" Jake was almost afraid to ask.

Nog stood at the edge of a break in the ledge. It was almost two meters from Nog's right foot to where the ledge continued. Normally, Jake thought, it would not be that difficult a jump, but there was no room on the narrow ledge to take a running start—and hardly any room on the other side for even a small misstep.

There were some rocks sticking out that they could grab onto after the jump, if they made it—and if the rocks didn't break off.

After talking it over, they decided that Jake would go first. Even if he didn't have the advantage of Nog's eyesight, he was the better athlete of the two. Not only would he have a better chance of making the jump and hanging on, he could also help Nog when the Ferengi made a try.

Nog moved back while Jake planned how to make the jump. His father had taught him that a great athlete is first of all a smart athlete. He knew that he wouldn't get the chance to try again, for any mistake would send him crashing down to the rocky canyon floor.

Finally he stepped to the edge of the break, then backed off three short steps. That would have to be enough to propel him across the void. Jake had made much broader jumps, but he was sweating despite the cold evening.

"Don't take all day," Nog urged impatiently.

"I'll take all the time I need," Jake replied. "There won't be a retry if this doesn't work."

"Sorry," Nog apologized. "I'm nervous, too."

Jake took a deep breath, then let it out slowly. He was as ready as he would ever be. "Here goes the galaxy," he said, mimicking the words of the Rocket Rangler, his favorite holosuite hero. Jake took a running start . . . one step . . . two . . . three—

—and he was off and leaping across the void.

For a moment that seemed to stretch to eternity. Jake was certain he had misjudged the jump. He knew he wasn't going to make it.

Then he hit solid ground. He was across the void and on the ledge on the other side. But, indeed, he had misjudged his jump—and leaped too far. The wall here was smooth, there were no rocks to grab onto—and he fell backward over the edge.

This was where Jake's athletic abilities, all of his training in the holosuite under his father's watchful eye, paid off. He twisted as he fell and managed to grab onto the ledge.

"Jake!" Nog yelled out in desperation as he saw his friend start to fall.

"Okay—" Jake gasped as he hung onto the ledge and slowly pulled himself up. "I'm okay."

After taking a couple minutes to relax, Jake moved close to the break in the ledge. He found a good solid handhold in the rock and then yelled, "Nog. It's your turn."

Nog's courage, which was not very deep to begin with, had vanished after seeing his friend's jeopardy. He hesitated. "I'm not ready."

It was getting very dark. "Come on," Jake encouraged him. "You have to do it now. I can catch you on this side."

Nog continued to hesitate. This whole venture up the canyon wall had been his idea, and now he was convinced it was going to end badly. "I can't . . ."

"Yes, you can. You're afraid."

"No, I'm not."

"Yes, you are. So was I. But you have to do this. You have to face your fear and leap through it."

Nog laughed as he heard the familiar words of their holosuite companion. "That's the Rocket Rangler talking." But this wasn't an illusion, this was real.

"Maybe. But it's the truth."

Nog continued to hesitate. Finally Jake said, "I'm getting tired and cold. If you don't jump now, I'm going into the cave and leave you dangling out here all night."

Both of them knew that Jake would never do that. He would have stayed on his side of the ledge all night if he had to, but it was enough to spur Nog into action.

Moving quickly, so he wouldn't have time to reconsider his actions, Nog stepped to the edge and leaped across.

He hit the ledge with less than a centimeter to spare, but it was enough. Jake used his free hand to haul his friend in against the canyon wall while anchoring himself with his other hand. Nog slammed against the rock hard, but Jake was able to keep the Ferengi from bouncing backward and off the ledge.

"That was easy," Jake said when he was certain they were safe.

"Easy for you to say. My ears are ringing. Next time I have an idea like this, talk me out of it."

Jake laughed. They both laughed. What might have happened was forgotten.

In the pale light from Eden's twin moons, they cautiously made their way along the ledge until finally they were standing directly over the cave entrance.

Jake had always found that climbing down was more difficult than climbing up. This was true now as he carefully knelt and lowered himself over the edge and began to descend.

"There's a place for your foot just to your right," Nog advised him, and Jake found it. He found another handhold just below the ledge and let himself drop down. One more step—and Jake was able to drop down onto the rocky shelf that led into the cave.

With less hesitation than before, Nog quickly but carefully followed his friend. In a few moments they were both peering into the black interior of the rock cave.

The night wind was beginning to pick up as they entered the shelter of the cave. It became warmer as they moved farther into the interior. Not comfortably warm, as in his quarters on Deep Space Nine, but more bearable that it would have been had they remained outside.

They had taken less than a dozen steps when Nog's foot crunched on something. He stopped to pick it up.

"What is it?" Jake asked.

"I don't think you want to know," Nog replied as he held the object up so that it caught the wan light streaming through the cave entrance.

Jake looked at the object, then took it from Nog's hand and felt it. Nog was right. He didn't want to know what it was.

What Jake held in his hand was a piece of bone that something had obviously feasted upon. And the moistness told Jake that it had not been very long ago.

CHAPTER 10

There were other bone fragments scattered around this part of the cave. They had no idea if the something, or more than one something, that had done the eating was still there.

Neither of the boys wanted to stay and find out what might inhabit the cave, but it was cold and dark outside, so they had little choice. Cautiously they moved deeper, stopping when they found a small notch just big enough for the two of them a few meters above the cave floor.

They decided that one would sleep while the other remained awake—in case. They didn't want to go into detail about the "in case."

Nog slept first, crawling behind Jake to where there was room to stretch out. Jake envied Nog's ability to fall asleep easily. Now that they weren't on the move, he realized that he had never been so thirsty in his life. The yearning for adventure that the Fjori ship had stimulated was now dampened by the reality of their situation. What might be a wonderful game in a holosuite was a lot less fun when it actually happened.

Two hours later Jake poked his Ferengi friend and woke him. "Your turn."

After some sleepy grumbles, Nog switched places with Jake. Being taller than Nog, Jake found it more difficult to find a comfortable position. But he was more tired than he realized and quickly he was fast asleep.

Jake dreamed of being back on Deep Space Nine, of being in bed in his own quarters.

Nog was supposed to waken Jake two hours later. But when something caused Jake to open his eyes, he saw that it was daylight outside the cave.

"Nog, why didn't you wake me?" Jake saw why, even as he asked the question—his friend was asleep, his ears twitching the way Ferengi ears twitched when they were dreaming.

Jake nudged Nog to wake up. Now that it was daylight outside, they needed to get moving. Nog stirred, but his eyes remained closed. Jake nudged him harder, then stopped short. He heard it again. The sound that had awoken him.

It was coming from deeper in the cave. A kind of soft padding. Something was in the cave with them—and it was coming in their direction.

"Nog," Jake whispered in his friend's ear, and pushed him hard. Nog almost tumbled off the notch in the cave wall, but Jake kept hold of him as the Ferengi bolted upright.

"What?" Nog was not quite fully awake.

"Something's coming," Jake whispered.

Nog heard it, and now he was wide awake.

Together they leaped down from the notch and landed on the cave floor. There was enough light spilling in from the entrance that they could see all the bones littering the ground. They had stumbled into something's kitchen, and whatever it was, it had a voracious appetite.

Behind them, deeper in the cave, the padding was growing louder. They heard a roar—and then they saw the beast. It was like an Earth bear in appearance, except it had scales instead of fur, and the claws were terrible to behold.

The boys scrambled for the cave entrance. The beast was right behind him, but it was not running. It seemed to sense that its newfound prey had no chance of escaping.

Outside the cave, Jake and Nog found themselves on the narrow lip of rock below the ledge. And they found that they had forgotten something important when they dropped down from the ledge. There was no way to climb back up. The rock wall of the canyon was too slick.

"There must be another way into the cave," Jake said, realizing they had come in through the "back door," which was why they hadn't encountered the beast before. It probably only came back to this end when it was ready to eat—and now it was planning on having the two boys for breakfast.

Jake suddenly had the awful realization they had

two choices—jump and probably get killed when they landed on the rocks below, or stay and be eaten alive.

Commander Benjamin Sisko woke up sweating.
He had had a nightmare. His son was in danger, and there was nothing he could do about it. The feeling was like those terrible moments during the battle of Wolf 359 when his starship, the *Saratoga,* was coming

apart. His wife, Jennifer, had already been killed by a direct hit from the Borg ship. The *Saratoga*'s reactors had gone critical and the ship was about to self-destruct. For what seemed like hours, Benjamin Sisko had been unable to locate Jake.

Then, with what could only be described as a miracle, he heard Jake's voice through the noise and chaos. He found his son unhurt but pinned under wreckage. With strength born of desperation, Sisko was able to move the twisted steel enough so that Jake could crawl out. Together, they had escaped in the shuttle, even as the *Saratoga* exploded behind them.

Now, as he sat in his darkened quarters, Sisko thought he could hear his son calling out to him again—only this time there was nothing he could do.

Jake was indeed calling out, but his voice was directed at Nog, who hesitated at the edge when he looked down at the canyon floor below them. "I can't," Nog said. "It's too far down. We'll be killed."

"You're probably right, but we have no choice." The beast was getting nearer. Jake would rather take the chance that he'd only break his leg than become a meal for some alien creature.

Nog grabbed Jake's hand. "Then we do it together." They stepped to the edge and were about to leap out into space—when they heard a familiar voice.

"Jake. Nog. Grab hold."

Looking up at the top of the cliff, they saw Vija

peering over the edge. She had tossed down a rope. Jake grabbed the rope and pulled it to him. He saw that it had knots every meter so that it could be used for climbing.

"Go," he ordered Nog, who needed no encouragement as he quickly began to climb.

The beast emerged from the cave and swatted at Jake as he started up the rope behind Nog. Jake felt something slash his leg as he tried to pull himself up out of reach of the beast's claws.

Ignoring the sharp sensation of pain, Jake continued to climb. In a few minutes he had reached the top and Nog was helping him up onto solid ground.

"Thanks," Jake was able to say to Vija before collapsing from the pain.

For what seemed like an eternity, Jake lay on the stone roof of the canyon in a kind of slow-motion fog, while Vija ministered to the ugly gash in his leg. Now that the adrenaline from the escape was no longer pumping through his veins, the pain multiplied.

Vija used a rather primitive, by Federation standards, med-probe to seal the wound. "Fortunately, it is not deep," she told Nog. Then she froze the wound area to reduce the pain.

"How are you feeling?" Vija asked.

With the pain subsiding, Jake was able to sit up. "Better," he mumbled.

"Drink this." Vija handed him a water container, and Jake quickly took several large gulps and started to cough.

"Slowly," Vija cautioned.

Jake took her advice and took another long, slow drink. Then he returned the container to Vija. "Keep it," she said. "I have another."

Jake fastened the container to his belt under his tunic. Now he stood up on still shaky legs, assisted by Nog, and looked around. They were on the top of the canyon. Behind them was the desert and the village. On the other side of the canyon was a flat plateau that led toward the mountains. Directly between them and the mountains was a dense swamp, a kind of huge oasis that had gone bad. Vija had told them that it was a place to be avoided if at all possible.

"How close behind us are Kala and the others?" Jake asked.

"Close enough that we have to start moving," Vija replied.

"I'm glad you followed us," Jake told her. "But aren't you breaking Fjori tradition by helping us?"

"Perhaps, a little. But this test is really unfair, and you deserve what you Terrans call 'a level playing field.'"

Nog looked up at the sky and the mountains beyond. "It will be dark before we reach the mountains." Jake looked up at the sun and saw from its position that it was almost noon. He hadn't realized that his injury had lost them at least a precious hour.

"Yes," Vija agreed with Nog. "Starting at dawn there would have been time. Now we will have to spend the night in the swamp."

"The swamp?" Jake questioned. "Didn't you tell us that we should avoid taking that path?"

"Yes. I did, and we should. But we have no choice now."

As they started to move out, Jake noticed that even Vija's self-confidence was somewhat shaken by the prospect of traveling through the swamp at night. *What,* he wondered, *is waiting for us in there?*

CHAPTER 11

Vija knew a short cut down the backside of the canyon. Jake realized that she must have undertaken the ritual herself, not many years ago.

"Did you go through the swamp on your trek?" Jake asked as they crossed the broad plateau. He knew they could still use an alternate route.

"No," Vija admitted. "But I have visited the place with my father," she added quickly. "I know the dangers and how to avoid them."

"Won't Kala follow us into the swamp?" Nog wondered.

"No. He will think that a *gajo* would not dare attempt such a route. He would also believe that you would never leave the swamp if you entered."

At that moment, in the canyon, that was exactly what Kala and the trackers believed as they followed the trail. Trax, who lead the trackers, decided to break into two teams. "One will follow the plateau to the mountains, and I will lead three men along the old riverbed."

"And what if they take the swamp?" someone asked.

Kala laughed. "Then that is their bad luck. However," he said to Trax, "there is an easier way to catch the *gajos.*"

"Which is?"

"To set a trap for them—just in case they reach the nest of the Graf."

"Kala, you're beginning to think like a dirtsider," Trax barked. "That is not the Fjori way. We track them as the ritual demands."

Kala nodded. "You're right. The test must be fair— even for *gajos.*"

The swamp was not quite what Jake had expected. It was not wetlands, but more like mudlands. Geysers spit up hot ash and smoke, and it was like walking through the aftermath of a volcanic eruption. The trees that remained were gnarled and twisted and petrified into stone. Purple weeds crawled along the hot earth and occasionally clustered into dense forest patches. Vija took special care to avoid those places where the weeds were thickest. Jake asked her why.

"The weeds are like the web of the Hjono spider. A few are no problem, but when they join in clusters they can squeeze the life of an animal—or a person."

"Killer weeds," Nog mumbled to himself. He wondered if there might be a market for such foliage, which would make great watchplants when they got back to Deep Space Nine. *If* they got back, he corrected himself as they walked deeper into this forbidding landscape.

It had been two hours since they entered the swamp. Vija said it would take five hours to cross. Looking up at the sky, Jake estimated they had another hour, perhaps two, before sunset.

"Wouldn't it be better to continue and camp when we're past the swamp?" Jake asked.

Vija shook her head. "No. It is too dangerous to travel through here in darkness. We might run into a *pviat.*" The way she spoke the word made Jake feel that the last thing he would want to encounter in the darkness would be a pviat, whatever that was.

They paused at a small sinkhole and Vija was able to filter enough water to fill her container. They each had several swallows. It tasted terrible, but Vija said it was safe to drink, and their thirst overcame their reservations.

When it was almost sunset, Vija stopped and pointed off to the left. "That is where we will stay the night."

It was an indentation in the ground surrounded on three sides by purple weeds. "I thought we should avoid those things," Nog said.

"Those are not the same as the others. See the roots. These are weak and will not entangle us."

Jake looked, but he wasn't certain he could tell the difference. As he followed Vija into the open area, some of the weeds seemed to reach out for him, but it was a feeble attempt. Still, he did not like the thought of spending the night surrounded by something that was like a web of a Hjono spider.

Once the trio was settled inside the area, Vija took out her knife and cut three large leaves from a brownish shrub that grew near the roots of the purple weeds. She handed one leaf to Jake, another to Nog, and kept the third. "Dinner."

Jake looked at the strange leaf, which felt rather slimy as he held it. "I'm not much of a salad eater."

Vija took a bite of the leaf and swallowed quickly. "It will nourish you. Eat."

Jake followed her example and bit off a piece from his leaf. It tasted even worse than it looked, but he managed to gulp it down. Somehow he finished off almost all the leaf. Nog, who was not as selective in his choice of diet, devoured his leaf. Then he ate what Jake had left of his.

Darkness came quickly when the sun set. The three of them sat back-to-back-to-back so that they could share body warmth and be able to see danger that might stalk them from any direction.

It turned out to be a long night. There were strange noises from things that moved through the swamp. Once, Jake thought he saw something running past them, but he was half asleep and wasn't certain.

Neither Jake or Nog slept all that well, and when the first traces of dawn's light fell over the swamp, they were anxious to move on.

As they started to exit their camping area, Jake noticed Vija picking up something from the ground. "What's that?" he asked.

Vija showed him a small round crystal. It was blue-white and vibrated. "This is a bumper. It emits sounds that are programmed to keep pviats and other creatures at a distance."

"You should have told us we had nothing to worry about," Nog said.

"I could have. But then you would not have stayed alert." Vija pocketed the crystal. "Besides, the bumper does not always work."

Two hours later they left the swamp and were standing at the base of the mountains. Vija pointed to a peak two hundred meters above them. "There is a Graf nest up there. I will wait for you near the dry river." She proceeded to scratch out a crude map in the dirt.

Jake and Nog then started toward the rocks. It was a steep ascent, but there were plenty of handholds and resting points, so it would not be too difficult a climb. Vija watched them until they were about a quarter of the way to their destination, then turned and started off toward their rendezvous place.

As predicted, Jake found the climb wasn't particularly difficult, but it was tiring and they rested every dozen meters or so. Finally, the peak was in sight.

"Let's hope that no one's home," Nog said, wanting to get this over with as fast as possible and return to solid ground.

Suddenly a shadow swooped over them. They ducked and Jake nearly lost his balance. Circling the peak above them they saw what must be the Graf.

A prehistoric flying dinosaur from Old Earth was what came to Jake's mind. The Graf was the size of the California condors he had seen in school's nature program, with great leathery wings, sharp talons, and a bone-crushing beak. *A formidable obstacle,* Jake thought as he wondered how they were going to get past.

Fortunately, they were just below the peak, where the rocks slanted inward, and the Graf had not seen them. But it would certainly spot them when they ventured closer to its nest.

"I'm not sure this is worth it," Nog said. "I prefer Ferengi rituals. You might lose a fortune, but not your life."

"We've come too far to quit," Jake replied with as much bravery as he could muster. "Put some of that Ferengi smartness to work. We need a plan."

"That's simple. One of us has to be bait, while the other grabs a feather."

"And I suppose you want me to be the bait?"

Nog shook his head. "No. I'll do it, while you go for the nest."

Jake was surprised at Nog's choice, until he realized that Nog could take cover from the Graf in a cavity in the rock a few meters below them. He, on the other hand, would have to climb quickly, grab a feather from the nest, and return before the Graf spotted him—without the benefit of shelter.

But he was the better climber and Nog's plan did make sense. He didn't have to like it.

Nog lowered himself down to the cavity, made certain he was protected, then began yelling loudly.

It didn't take long for the Graf to come swooping down toward Nog. The bird, more curious than aggressive, zoomed past where Jake was hiding. He was amazed at the size of the bird close up. For a moment he thought about giving up the test, then began climbing as fast as he could.

Jake did not look back to see if Nog was keeping the Graf occupied. He really didn't want to know, and so he concentrated on crossing the last few meters to the nest as quickly as possible.

Inside the nest were three oval eggs about the size of baseballs. *How could anything that big hatch from eggs that small?* he wondered. But he didn't pause to reflect on the marvels of nature. He reached into the nest and scooped up a single feather.

Jake was just starting down when a whoosh of wings made him realize he was no longer alone—the Graf, obviously tired of playing games with Nog, was coming straight at him.

Tucking the feather inside his tunic, Jake jumped down to the ledge below and, misjudging the distance, slipped off—and tumbled out into space.

Frantically, Jake reached out for something—for anything. The first rock he grabbed onto broke away, but it slowed his fall just enough so that the next ledge he hit he was able to hang onto.

Barely. For as his fingers dug into the loose stone, Jake could feel himself slipping. Then, when he was about to lose his grip, a hand closed around his wrist.

Nog was on the ledge, trying to pull him up. With a final burst of effort, Jake pushed against the mountain wall and vaulted up onto the ledge.

"Can't you ever do anything the easy way?" Nog chided once they were safe.

"The Graf?" Jake asked.

Nog pointed to the sky above the peak as Jake looked up and saw the great reptilian bird circling high in the sky over its nest, no longer interested in them.

"The feather?" Nog asked.

Jake reached under his tunic, afraid for a moment he had lost what they had come so far to find, but it was still there. "This is our ticket home," he said, showing it to Nog, then tucked it away again. "Now let's go find Vija."

Their spirits high from their success, they made the climb down in half the time it had taken them to reach the peak. They were almost giddy with excitement as they made their way to the dry river where Vija promised to meet them.

Eden's sun was low in the sky when they arrived at their destination. But Vija was not there. Instead someone else was waiting for them—Kala. And in his hand, aimed directly at them, was a phaser.

CHAPTER 12

Game's over and you lose," Kala said with a smile as he fingered the phaser he held menacingly in his hand.

"How'd you find us?" Nog wanted to know.

Kala pulled a long-range scope from his belt. "I was following you all the way up the mountain—from a distance."

"You're not supposed to be using that," Jake said angrily.

"You play by your rules, I'll play be mine. What matters is that a couple of *gajos* like you don't pass the ritual."

"Even if you have to resort to a phaser," Jake retorted.

Kala looked at the weapon in his hand, then slowly knelt and set it on the ground. "I don't need this to defeat you two."

Nog, taking a fighting stance, stepped forward, but Jake held him back. "No, Nog. This is between Kala and me."

"So it is," Kala said, and he walked toward Jake.

Jake, trying to remember the Klingon fighting techniques he had practiced in the holosuites back on Deep Space Nine, met him halfway. The two circled each other, sizing up the other's strengths and weaknesses.

Kala was older, with a distinct weight advantage, and he was obviously streetwise. That was part of the Fjori mystique. On the other hand, Jake was the son of a Starfleet officer and had been taught to avoid a confrontation whenever possible, but to know how to win when a fight was the only way out.

Suddenly Kala swung out his right arm and threw an almost clumsy punch, which Jake easily avoided. But what he didn't avoid, or anticipate, was Kala's left leg striking like a snake and smashing into his leg. Kala hit the spot where Jake had been gashed by the beast in the cave. Kala saw the potential weak spot and went after it.

Sharp waves of pain stung Jake and he momentarily lost balance. Kala kicked again, this time catching Jake in the stomach and doubling him over as he collapsed to the ground on his knees.

Hurt and dizzy, Jake sensed Kala moving in for the final blow. But as the Fjori's fist slammed down toward the back of his neck, Jake willed himself to move—and rolled out of the path, Kala's fist connecting with thin air.

The Fjori whirled for another attack—just as Jake threw himself head first into Kala and the two tumbled backward onto the ground. Realizing that he was no match for Kala's kick-boxing offense, Jake determined to use the Ferengi wrestling techniques Nog had taught him. Ferengis are a small race and not noted for their speed and dexterity, so they have learned to rely on a close-contact wrestling strategy that uses their opponents' weak points.

Kala, the stronger of the two, rolled Jake onto his back and tried to pin him. But that was exactly what Jake had anticipated, and he struck Kala just below the armpit with his open left hand. The Fjori's neck snapped back, and Jake pushed him off and then grasped the Fjori's neck in a very vulnerable spot.

"Give up," Jake commanded.

Kala tried to struggle, but Jake's hold was firm. A quick twist and Kala would have been unconscious, but Jake didn't want that. "Give up," he said again, increasing the pressure.

"Yield." Kala had enough. "I yield."

Jake released Kala and jumped back. There was a moment as the flush returned to the Fjori when it appeared he would resume the battle, then that moment passed. "You fought me bravely and won, Jake Sisko. I do not like to lose, especially to a *gajo,* but this victory is yours."

Nog came over and grabbed Jake's arm. "Come on, Jake. We need to get moving before the rest of the trackers get here."

"Your friend's right," Kala said. "I took a shortcut because I knew you'd come this way. They are close behind me."

"So let's go," Nog urged.

"We can't," Jake said. "Not until we find Vija."

"Vija?" Kala jumped to his feet. "What are you talking about?"

"She was supposed to meet us here," Jake said.

"She helped you on the ritual?" Kala demanded.

Jake nodded. "I guess we both cheated a little."

Kala was suddenly upset. "She is in danger."

"How do you know that?"

"Because—I set a trap. I expected you two to fall into it. But she must have taken the path ahead of you—and become the victim."

Twilight lasts on Eden for only minutes. It was already dark as the three made their way back toward the mountains. Fortunately, there was moonlight and Kala's scope had a night vision lens.

"What kind of trap did you set?" Jake asked Kala.

"A simple one. This area is full of sand pits."

"I know. Vija told us. You can tell them by the light-colored ground."

"Yes. But I covered several of them with regular dirt. They would not be noticed, particularly by someone who is in a hurry."

"So Vija could have fallen into one of them."

"She must have. But she should be all right. It would difficult to climb out, but not impossible. I only wanted to slow you down so you would not get back in time."

Jake started to say something unpleasant to Kala, but Nog had made a discovery. "Over here."

They ran to where Nog was standing. The ground at his feet was a mixture of light-colored sand and darker dirt. Lying at the very edge was the crystal device that Vija called a bumper. "Vija's buried in there," Jake shouted.

"The pit was deeper than I thought," Kala wailed. "She couldn't get out before it pulled her down."

Jake recalled what Vija had told him about the sand

pits. If you fell into one, she said, you pushed yourself to the edge where there the ground was solid and climbed up. The sand was porous and you would be able to breathe for—he forgot how long she had said.

"She's in there and we have to go after her."

"It's too late."

"No." Jake refused to believe that. He ran over and pulled some leathery vines from the bushes that clung to the rocks. "Help me."

"What're you doing?" Nog wondered, even as he helped pull out some vines.

Jake began to tie the vines together. "The pit must expand underground. It's probably too wide for Vija to reach the edge. Someone's going to have to pull me out." Jake tied one end of the vine around his waist.

Kala was now helping, and they had several meters length of vine. "I hope this is long enough," Nog said.

"I only hope it holds together," Jake replied, then stepped into the sand pit and began to sink into the liquidlike ground.

Before he could have second thoughts, Jake was submerged in a sandy darkness. His first impulse was total panic. He couldn't see and he couldn't breathe. He was being buried alive.

But then he realized, even as he continued to sink, that he could breathe. Not well, but there was air captured within the sand pit. He could stay alive in here for a long time, which would probably be a worse fate than a quick drowning.

He tried to swim, reaching out, hoping to find Vija.

He had only his sense of touch to rely upon. As he twisted and turned, he even lost his sense of direction.

Then suddenly he hit something. He thought at first it was the edge of the pit where the ground became solid, but this was softer. It was like—it was an arm. He had found Vija.

Desperately, he pulled on the vine even as he grabbed Vija's belt. He waited, but there was no response. He pulled again, and this time there was a response. Slowly, he and Vija were being pulled up toward the surface.

Jake's head broke through the sand and he gulped in fresh air. He pushed Vija's head up. She was motionless as he handed her to Kala. They were too late.

Nog helped Jake out of the pit. It was brighter. Had he lost his sense of time and been in the pit all night? No. He saw a flare that lit up the area. "Kala set off a distress signal," Nog explained.

They were now joined by the other trackers, who had seen the signal. "What's going on?" Trax demanded.

Kala sobbed uncontrollably as he huddled over Vija's still form. "Sand pit. She's dead."

CHAPTER 13

Trax pushed Kala aside and knelt beside Vija. The Fjori felt her pulse. "No," he said. "She's not dead. She's put herself into coma. We need to get her back to the village." He pulled a communicator from his belt and activated the emergency beacon.

While an air-car sped Vija back to the village, Trax and the other trackers accompanied Jake and Nog in a slower tanklike ground vehicle. Kala, who was deeply upset by the incident, was allowed to return in the air-car. "He'll have some powerful explaining to do the captain," Trax remarked.

"Will Vija be all right?" Jake asked again, not yet having received an adequate answer to his question. He had no idea what it meant to put oneself into a coma.

Trax, who seemed to have mellowed a bit in his hostility to the *gajos,* tried to explain. "The Fjori have roamed the galaxy for centuries. During that time, we've picked up a few 'tricks' from the natives, most of whom are a lot more intelligent than the primary powers in the starlanes give them credit for being. The coma is a healing ritual. When the body is in crisis, like from a wound or a sickness, the very best medicine is time and rest so it can heal itself. But there isn't always time, and that's where the coma effect comes in."

Jake's eyes brightened. "I think I understand. People on Earth practice an ancient meditation called yoga. Some of the experts can slow their bodies down."

"I've read reports of some being buried in the ground for hours, but slowing their breathing process so they emerged with no harm," Nog added.

"That's it exactly, lads." Trax almost allowed himself to smile at them. "You did well on the ritual. I'm almost sorry you had to fail."

It was not until that moment that Jake realized that by staying behind to save Vija, he had lost his one chance of ever returning home. But even knowing that, he would not have done it any other way.

The tank vehicle arrived at the village at dawn. Jake and Nog stepped out to be greeted by a very much alive and well Vija and her father. She hugged both of them. "Thank you for saving my life."

"What about Kala?" Jake asked Captain Vardk.

"He will have to do penance for setting the trap. He did not intend harm, but it almost cost a life."

"It did keep us from finishing the ritual and getting home again." Jake added.

"Great-Grandmother's back from retreat," Vija

said with a hopeful smile. "Perhaps she can find a way out of this mess."

"Perhaps she can," Vardk said. "The council meets at noon, and we will know then."

At noon the council gathered. Great-Grandmother, who Jake thought must have been two hundred years old, sat in the center of the group. While she appeared frail from the passage of years, she seemed to have a core of hard steel deep inside. Her voice was soft, almost a whisper, and yet it commanded great respect.

"I have heard all that happened," Great-Grandmother began. She was addressing Jake and Nog, as well as almost all of the villagers who had gathered this time to witness. "What you boys did on Deep Space Nine violated our laws. But what some of our Fjori did was equally a violation." She looked at Trax and Kala, who lowered their heads.

"Two wrongs must become a single right," Great-Grandmother continued. She looked at Jake. "Do you have the feather of the Graf?"

Jake nodded and reached beneath his tunic. The feather was missing. He must have lost it in all that happened after the Graf attack, lost the proof that they had completed their quest.

Before Jake could try to explain, Kala stepped forward. "I have the feather, which Jake Sisko gave me for safekeeping." He handed the Graf feather to Jake, whispering in his ear, "You dropped it during the fight. I picked it up—and planned to keep it. But you won this rightfully, just as you won the fight."

"Thanks," Jake said. He took the feather from Kala, then stepped forward to place it on the council table directly in front of Great-Grandmother.

She picked up the feather with fingers gnarled by age, yet still strong and firm. She looked at Jake in silence for a long moment before she finally spoke. "Though you are offworlders and alien to the Fjori tradition, you performed well in the ritual." She glanced over at where Vija stood next to her father. "Though I understand you had some help."

Jake nodded.

"So technically you did not pass the Rite of Passage," Great-Grandmother continued. "The Fjori is bound by tradition, and there can be no exceptions, even for the most noble of reasons, else the whole fabric of our lives might unravel." She looked closely at Jake. "You understand this, do you not, young Sisko?"

Jake nodded again. He didn't like it, but he did understand the importance of their laws. His father had told him that without laws, no civilization could hope to survive. "I understand."

"So, you and your Ferengi friend cannot join the Fjori family through the Rite of Passage."

Nog, who had stepped up next to Jake, started to protest, but Great-Grandmother threw him a stern glance that made him hold his tongue.

Great-Grandmother motioned for Captain Vardk to approach the council table. "There is, however, another path to acceptance within the Fjori." She looked at Vardk. "Do you accept this obligation?"

"I do," he replied, then looked at Jake and Nog. "But you two will have to also accept."

"What're we accepting?" asked Nog.

"That the captain, my grandson, adopts you into his family."

"That makes us Fjori?" Jake asked.

"Yes," Vardk replied. "And because you are Fjori, it

also allows you to leave Eden and return to Deep Space Nine. But you will be bound by oath to never reveal the existence of this planet."

"We can agree to that." Jake turned to Nog. "Can't we?"

It was a struggle, since any knowledge of the Fjori would boost his standing with his uncle Quark, but Nog reluctantly agreed.

The formal adoption ceremony was held that afternoon. It was a brief but moving ritual, and when it was over, Jake and Nog met the members of their new "family." It was a much different welcome than their original appearance on Eden. There was a banquet, and Nog ate too much, while Jake found the Fjori music inspiring enough to ask Vija for a dance.

Finally, as night fell, a star-range scout ship was made ready for launch. Jake and Nog walked with Vija toward the airlock, happy they were going home. "I'm only unhappy about one thing," Jake told Vija.

"What's that?"

"That now you're my 'sister.'"

"It is a sacrifice we both have to make." She smiled, leaned close and kissed Jake lightly on the cheek. "Don't forget me, Jake Sisko."

Before Jake could respond, Vija turned and vanished into the night. The airlock on the scout ship swung open to reveal Kala. "Going to stand around all night?"

"You're flying us to Deep Space Nine?" Nog asked.

"It's my penance. It's also my pleasure," he added with a smile.

Jake and Nog climbed into the ship. "Captain Vardk has sent a message through our trading channels. They know on Deep Space Nine that you're coming home."

"If I know my father, he'll throw a welcome home party." Jake sat down in a control chair next to Kala. "I'd like it if you could stay long enough to join us."

Kala smiled as he started the launch routine. "It would be my pleasure." When the computer signaled ready, Kala hit the main thrusters.

Slowly the scout ship rose from Eden's surface. Then, as it broke through the planet's atmosphere, the main rockets fired and the small craft lurched as it zoomed out into the dark interstellar night. Ahead of them was Gamma Quadrant, the wormhole, the Bajoran solar system, and Deep Space Nine—home.

About the Author

TED PEDERSEN began his career as a computer programmer in Seattle before making the trek south to Hollywood, where he has been writing animation, most recently for the *X-Men, Spider-Man,* and *Exo-Squad* TV series. His young adult books include a previous Deep Space Nine novel, *The Pet,* and the CyberSurfers series. He has also written "Internet for Kids," an introduction to the Internet. Ted and his wife, Phyllis, live in Venice, California, and share their home with several computers and cats.

About the Illustrator

TODD CAMERON HAMILTON is a self-taught artist who has resided all his life in Chicago, Illinois. He has been a professional illustrator for the past ten years, specializing in fantasy, science fiction, and horror. Todd is the current president of the Association of Science Fiction and Fantasy Artists. His original works grace many private and corporate collections. He has co-authored two novels and several short stories. When not drawing, painting, or writing, his interests include metalsmithing, puppetry, and teaching.

Join The **Star Trek**® Fan Club

MEMBERSHIP INCLUDES

➤ A year's subscription to the Official *Star Trek Communicator* Magazine, covering the very latest information on your favorite interplanetary explorers!

➤ A bi-monthly merchandise section in the magazine where you can buy your favorite Star Trek memorabilia

➤ An exclusive Star Trek membership kit

FOR MORE INFORMATION ON HOW YOU CAN JOIN WRITE TO

Official *Star Trek* Fan Club
P.O. Box 111000
Aurora, CO 80042

Or call: 1-800 TRUE-FAN.

<u>Tell your parent's that it's a free call!</u>